GEORGE E. STANLEY

Teddy Kennedy

LION OF THE

SENATE

Illustrated by Patrick Faricy

ALADDIN

New York   London   Toronto   Sydney

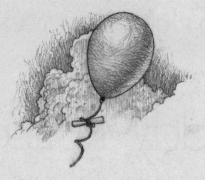

ALADDIN
An imprint of Simon & Schuster Children's Publishing Division
1230 Avenue of the Americas, New York, NY 10020
First Aladdin paperback edition March 2010
Text copyright © 2010 by George E. Stanley
Illustrations copyright © 2010 by Patrick Faricy
All rights reserved, including the right of reproduction
in whole or in part in any form.
ALADDIN is a trademark of Simon & Schuster, Inc.,
and related logo is a registered trademark of Simon & Schuster, Inc.
CHILDHOOD OF FAMOUS AMERICANS is a registered trademark
of Simon & Schuster, Inc.
For information about special discounts for bulk purchases,
please contact Simon & Schuster Special Sales at 1-866-506-1949
or business@simonandschuster.com.
The Simon & Schuster Speakers Bureau can bring authors to your live event.
For more information or to book an event contact
the Simon & Schuster Speakers Bureau at 1-866-248-3049
or visit our website at www.simonspeakers.com.
The text of this book was set in New Caledonia.
Manufactured in the United States of America 0710 OFF
2 4 6 8 10 9 7 5 3 1
Library of Congress Control Number 2010920247
ISBN 978-1-4169-9041-3
ISBN 978-1-4391-5821-0 (eBook)

Illustrations

CONTENTS

Teddy Kennedy

The Last Son

Rose Fitzgerald Kennedy looked out the window of her suite in St. Margaret's Hospital in Dorchester, Massachusetts.

Joseph Patrick Kennedy Sr. sat in a dark corner near the door.

In a cradle across the room, the new baby slept, a boy whom they had named Edward Moore Kennedy after Joe's longtime confidante and private secretary. He was their ninth child, four boys and five girls: Joseph Jr., John, Rosemary, Kathleen, Eunice,

Patricia, Robert, Jean, and now Teddy.

For a few minutes, Rose said nothing, preferring instead to watch the snow falling outside her window. It was February 22, 1932, the two hundredth anniversary of the birth of George Washington.

Then she let out a sigh. "It wasn't easy, Joe," she said. "I'm forty-one years old, and my friends all told me I was crazy to have another child, but . . ." She stopped and turned to face her husband.

"You'll have all the help you need with the children," Joe said, "and when you want to go to Europe, or wherever, then you'll have the money for that, too."

Rose turned away from her husband and back to the falling snow. A tear grew at the corner of one eye and fell down her cheek. She didn't bother to wipe it away.

Although the United States was suffering from a serious economic depression that had started in 1929, Joseph Kennedy had gotten out of the stock market before its collapse, thereby saving the Kennedy fortune, which had been made from banks, movies, and stocks.

Joe stood up. "I have to go back to New York City, Rose," he said. He looked at his pocket watch. "Will you be all right?"

"I'll be all right," she said. "Go on. Your driver is probably waiting for you."

"Are you sure?" Joe asked. "If the weather gets really bad, then I can take the train back up this weekend."

"I'm sure," Rose managed to say. "On your way out, would you please ask the Sister to come back in? I need something to help me sleep."

"Of course, dear," Joe said.

He came over and kissed her lightly on the cheek. She didn't respond.

Rose knew that Joe still couldn't understand why she had wanted to come to Boston for the child's birth. He had argued that there

were excellent medical facilities in New York. But Rose just had more confidence in her own doctor. After all, he had delivered the other eight children. And she had always felt more comfortable being in Boston than in their house in the Bronxville section of New York.

From her window, Rose had a view of the front of the hospital, and she had seen Joe's driver pull up to the entrance. He always had everything planned out, Joe did, down to the number of minutes he could stay with her. Still, he had given her everything she wanted and everything he had promised her father when he had asked him for his permission to marry his daughter. She watched Joe get into the automobile and the driver pull away from the curb. Slowly, she began to relax.

Rose knew that as the Depression had worsened, Joe had grown restless. Both her family and his had been active in politics in

Massachusetts, and there were people who thought Joseph Kennedy should run for president of the United States, but he had instead concentrated on making money, something at which he had been very successful. Still, politics seemed to be in the blood of both their families, and that year Joe would support the presidential candidacy of Franklin D. Roosevelt. He would raise money, and he would eventually help win over the support of William Randolph Hearst, a newspaper baron who controlled the Democratic National Convention delegates in both California and Texas. In doing so, Joe thought he would be rewarded with a major government appointment in Washington, D.C.

Suddenly, Rose opened her eyes. She couldn't understand why she was still in such pain.

Just then, the door opened. "Ah, you're awake," the nursing sister said. Rose adored this nun, Sister Genevieve. "When I came in to give you something to make you sleep," she said, "you were already sound asleep. I didn't want to wake you."

"Thank you, Sister," Rose said. "I think I need it now, though."

Sister Genevieve came closer. "You have a letter," she said. "Would you like to read it before I give you the medicine?"

"A letter?" Rose said.

Sister Genevieve nodded. "Shall I open it for you?" she asked.

"Please," Rose said.

Sister Genevieve slit the cream-colored envelope seal, took out a folded piece of note-paper, and handed it to Rose.

Right away, Rose recognized the hand-writing. It was from their second son, John, whom the family called "Jack." He was away at the Choate School in Connecticut. "He wants to be Teddy's godfather," Rose whispered. She handed the note back to Sister Genevieve. "He's only fourteen, but still he

7

wants to do this. He is such a thoughtful boy."

"You have a wonderful family, Mrs. Kennedy," Sister Genevieve said. She helped Rose sit up just long enough to receive the injection, and then she gently let her down and made sure she was covered warmly before she left the room.

Over the next two years, 1933 and 1934, Teddy became the freckle-faced pet of the family. His sister Jean started calling him "Biscuits and Muffins" because he was chubby and cheerful.

"You're the perfect little brother, Teddy," Eunice told him one day.

"Why?" Teddy asked.

"You don't argue as much as Joe," Kathleen said, "and you're more outgoing than Jack."

"And you're not as intense as Bobby," Rosemary said.

Teddy gave them all a puzzled look. "I don't understand what you mean," he said.

"Good! Keep it that way!" Patricia said. "We'll all be better off for it."

Although Joe and Rose loved their children, they didn't cuddle or coddle them. Instead, they held them to very high standards of behavior—all except Teddy. For some reason, from the beginning, they didn't seem to expect as much from him, and, because of that, neither Joe nor Rose pushed him as hard as they did their other children. In fact, sometimes they didn't push him at all.

We're Going to
See the King!

By 1935, when Teddy three years old, he
was more familiar with the governesses and
the servants who took care of the different
Kennedy households than he was with either
his mother or father.

Joe Kennedy was becoming more and more
involved with the administration of President
Franklin Delano Roosevelt in Washington,
D.C., while Rose Kennedy was often either

staying in her Manhattan apartment, so she could be closer to the shopping, dining with friends, and the theater, or traveling in Europe.

None of these arrangements seemed to create problems for the Kennedy children, however—Teddy included. They had been so instilled with a sense of purpose by their family that they were busy making their way in their own lives.

During this time, Joe Jr. and Teddy became almost like father and son. Teddy was a lovable child, and Joe Jr. didn't see his baby brother as a future threat to his privileges as the oldest son the way he saw both John and Robert.

In 1936, when Teddy was four years old, he began nursery school. While he enjoyed it, it seemed to pale when compared to the "schooling" he'd received as part of his large family. Still, he dived in each morning with as much gusto as he could. He'd already learned from his family how important it was to be competitive in everything he did.

One morning, when Marks, the family chauffeur, pulled up the circle drive of his school, Teddy noticed a couple of his classmates kicking a ball around on the grass. Right away, he knew what to do.

"Thank you, Marks," Teddy said as he opened the door. "I'll see you after school."

Before Marks could say anything, though, Teddy was out of the automobile and racing across the grass toward his classmates.

Teddy reached the first boy, whom he knew as Douglas, just as the boy pulled back his right leg to kick the ball to the other boy, whom Teddy knew as Benjamin. Without a word, Teddy let loose his most powerful kick, just like Joe Jr. had taught him, at the same time that Douglas's leg was ready to make contact.

Douglas's foot only met air, which sent him off balance, causing him to fall backward, but Teddy planted his foot right on the ball

and sent it sailing at almost supersonic speed toward Benjamin.

The ball hit Benjamin in the stomach, causing a whoosh of air to exit his mouth. After a few seconds of disbelief, Benjamin fell to the ground, screaming.

Just then, one of the principals of the school appeared, bell in hand, but she dropped the bell once she had seen what happened.

Now, Teddy was racing around the grounds, kicking and yelling for Benjamin and Douglas to get up. But they weren't paying any attention to him.

"Mr. Kennedy!" the principal shouted. "Come here at once!"

Teddy gave her a big grin and began kicking the ball toward where the principal was standing. Just as he reached the porch, two teachers came running out, one headed for Benjamin, the other for Douglas.

"May I please ask what in the world you think you're doing?" the principal said.

Teddy gave her a funny look. "What do you mean?" he asked.

The principal pursed her lips. "Why did you choose to injure your classmates?" she demanded.

"I just kicked the ball," Teddy said. He turned and looked at Douglas and Benjamin, who were being attended to by the teachers. "My brothers and sisters are always kicking the ball to me at home," Teddy explained. "Sometimes it hits me, and it really hurts, too."

"Oh, well, I guess you must know how Douglas and Benjamin feel then," the principal said.

Teddy nodded. "But I'm not allowed to fall on the ground and start crying," he said. "I'm expected to get back up and play even harder."

The principal just looked at Teddy for a few minutes, then said, "You don't say." With that, she turned and headed toward the door, but before she reached it, she turned back around and said, "This isn't your house, Mr. Kennedy. At this school, you will not behave that way. Do you understand?"

Teddy bowed his head. "Yes, ma'am," he said.

From that day on, none of his other classmates wanted to have anything to do with Teddy. In fact, they would giggle and whisper when he got close to them, then they would run off in the opposite direction. Teddy began to hate nursery school.

When he told Joe Jr. what had happened to him, he didn't receive any sympathy at all.

"You're a Kennedy, Teddy," Joe Jr. said. "If something bad happens to you, then you just turn it into something good. You don't start feeling sorry for yourself."

For some reason, though, Teddy wasn't able to rein in the competitiveness that was being instilled in him every day at home. Each day at nursery school, fewer and fewer boys would play with him. When Teddy decided to see if some of the girls would play with him, since that was what his sisters—especially Rosemary—did, they all ran off screaming.

One day, Teddy was so upset that he slipped out a bathroom window just before the end of the day and started walking home. It was one of the more pleasant experiences he could remember. In fact, he told himself, he might just start doing this until it got too cold.

Teddy finally reached his house right before dark. He saw two police cars parked in front. Thinking something bad had happened to one of his brothers or sisters, or even to one of his parents, he raced for the front door and burst inside.

Teddy immediately saw his mother sitting in a chair, her head bowed, her shoulders shaking, surrounded by Rosemary and Joe Jr.

When everyone turned to see who the intruder was, Joe Jr. cried, "Teddy! Where in the world have you been?"

"I walked home!" Teddy said, trying to sound as proud as he could. "It was fun!"

Rose Kennedy stood up. "Fun? You call worrying me to death *fun*? I couldn't imagine what had happened to you, Teddy. I expected the worst." She turned to the policemen. "Thank you for coming, officers, but I'll take it from here."

Teddy noticed that the two police officers were trying not to smile. They weren't having much luck. He was sure that they knew what he knew. He was going to be paddled.

Two weeks later, after Saturday mass, Rose told Teddy to change clothes, then to come to her sitting room, because she wanted to talk to him about Christ's Sermon on the Mount.

Teddy looked at Joe Jr. with pleading eyes, only to receive a rebuke from his brother's left eyebrow. He did as he was told, but he didn't hurry.

Finally, after he had exhausted every possible

excuse he could think of, Teddy knocked on the door of his mother's sitting room and opened it when he heard her say, "Come in."

Rose was sitting in her favorite love seat, under a wide window, and motioned for Teddy to join her.

When Teddy had made himself comfortable, leaning against his mother's left shoulder, Rose said, "The Sermon on the Mount is found in the fifth, sixth, and seventh chapters of Matthew, Teddy, and it is the greatest sermon that Jesus ever preached. It contains the beatitudes, the new laws, the Lord's Prayer, what a Christian's attitude toward money should be, and speaks of the dangers of false teachers and hypocrisy."

The room felt stuffy, and Teddy wanted to close his eyes, but he knew that would only prolong the lesson, so he stifled a yawn, and said, "I want to learn all I can, Mama."

For the next hour, Rose read the verses from Matthew, telling Teddy that the reason the beatitudes began with "blessed" was that they were meant to comfort Christian believers who were suffering. By the time Rose had reached the verses with the Lord's Prayer, Teddy had closed his eyes twice and yawned once.

Finally, Rose said, "Teddy, I can see your attention span is still rather short, so instead of continuing I'm going to stop and let you take a nap."

"Mama! I want to play!" Teddy cried. "Bobby said he'd throw the football to me."

"How can you play football if you can't stay awake?" Rose asked. She shook her head. "After you've rested, you may go outside." She stood up. "I'll let Bertha know that you have my permission to play outside when you wake up."

Teddy knew better than to argue. In fact, he was angry at himself. If he had only not yawned and kept his eyes open, he would be on his way outside at this very moment.

He'd remember to do that next time.

As Teddy headed up the stairs to his room, he passed Rosemary coming down.

"Teddy! I've been looking for you everywhere!" Rosemary said. "Do you want to play kickball?"

"I have to take a nap," Teddy said.

Rosemary's face dropped.

"I'm sorry, Rosemary," Teddy said. "Mama said I had to."

"All right," Rosemary said. "I'll kick the ball around by myself."

Teddy loved Rosemary, but there were times when he didn't understand her. She was so unlike the rest of his brothers and sisters. Their parents expected them all to enter every kind of competition open to them— athletic or scholarly—and they were expected to win. If they didn't, they were expected to practice harder, so they would win the next time. For some reason, none of this applied to Rosemary. When Teddy had asked why, he was told that Rosemary had special needs and that she wasn't able to compete in the same way the rest of them were. Teddy wasn't sure he understood exactly what that meant. Once, though, when he was playing with Rosemary and got too rough, Bobby took him aside and scolded him.

"You need to remember that some people are different from the rest of us, Teddy, and Rosemary is one of those people," Bobby said. "It's important that you learn to understand what they can do and what they can't."

As Teddy continued up the stairs, toward his bedroom, he vowed that he would be kinder and more understanding toward his sister. Still, he wondered why Rosemary was the way she was. *Why couldn't she have been like the rest of us?* he asked himself. He went to sleep thinking about it.

On Sundays, one of Teddy's favorite routines was having his father read the comics to him.

However, Joe Kennedy was away quite often, doing what he thought was necessary to support President Roosevelt. Joe hoped he would be appointed to an important post in Roosevelt's new administration. So, after his reelection in 1936, these Sunday morning pleasures were few and far between. But on this particular morning in early 1937, Joseph Kennedy had returned to the family's home.

Teddy had been warned by his mother to leave his father alone. When he dared to question her as to why, she said, "You wouldn't understand, dear."

A few minutes later, Teddy overheard Jack and Bobby talking about the same thing.

"After all our father has done for the president, he was only offered the head of the United States Maritime Commission," Jack said. "That's an insult to the family."

"Of course it is," Bobby said. "Father should have at least been offered one of the top-level posts."

Teddy continued on into the dining room where his father was finishing his coffee.

"Papa, will you read the comics to me?" Teddy asked.

Joe Kennedy's solemn expression changed almost immediately. "Of course I shall, Teddy," he said. "I always look forward to doing that."

Teddy found the comic pages and jumped into his father's lap. "I've missed you, Papa," he said.

Joe gave Teddy a hug. "I've missed you, too," he said.

For the next few hours, they read every one of the strips in the comic section. Some of them Teddy didn't really care about, but his father had a way of making them all come alive. Teddy especially enjoyed *Terry and the Pirates*.

"Read it again, Papa!" Teddy said.

All in all, that day, Joe Kennedy reenacted the story of young Terry and his adventures in exotic China five times—even with sound effects! Terry pitted himself against smugglers, thieves, and pirates. Even though Dragon Lady tried her best to outsmart him, she was never successful.

When Teddy asked his father to read the story a sixth time, Joe said, "Well, I need to make a telephone call first, Teddy." He looked at his watch. "Now that my political career seems to be over, I'll be leaving tomorrow morning for Hollywood. Reading *Terry and the Pirates* reminded me that I need to call a director friend of mine about a story I think would make a very good picture."

At the time, Teddy thought it might be fun to have his father in California again, so he could ride the train out to visit him. He'd love to see how movies were made.

It wasn't long after that, though, just a few weeks, when one of his sisters showed him a very flattering article about their father which appeared in *Fortune* magazine.

"This means Papa will probably go back into politics," Jack told Teddy. "President Roosevelt can't ignore him now."

Jack was right, Teddy soon learned. Within months, President Roosevelt named Joe Kennedy as the first-ever Irish-American ambassador to Great Britain.

"You'd better start packing, Teddy," Rosemary told him. "We're moving to London."

The American Prince

"Papa! Papa! Where are you?" six-year-old Teddy shouted. He was looking out the compartment window of the train that had brought them from Southampton, the port where their ship from New York had docked, to Waterloo Station in London. He stuck his nose against the pane and began waving frantically. "Papa! Papa! We're finally here! Where are you?"

After President Roosevelt had appointed his father ambassador to the Court of St.

James, which meant ambassador to Great Britain, Teddy knew that the whole family had planned to sail together, but his mother had suffered an attack of appendicitis, so his father sailed to London by himself.

Now, in March 1938, everyone else was coming, except for Joe and Jack, who were still in the United States. Teddy knew they'd be coming over in the summer, though, so he wasn't too unhappy!

When the train finally stopped, Teddy grabbed his small suitcase and started for the compartment door.

"Teddy, just where do you think you're going?" his nurse demanded.

"I'm going to find Papa," Teddy replied.

His sister Jean shook her head. "Not until we're all together, Teddy," she said. "Papa told Mama exactly how he wanted us to look stepping off the train."

Ever since finding out they were moving to London, the entire family had talked about how the British people were fascinated that a large Boston Irish family would be descending on the London diplomatic scene.

"A lot of the British people don't have too much respect for the Irish," Eunice had told them earlier. She raised an eyebrow and added, "It's up to our family to show them how civilized we can be!"

Teddy tried to contain himself, but he was finding it increasingly difficult. He really missed his father, and he could hardly wait to run into his arms and have his father lift him high into the sky.

As the train began to slow, Teddy pressed his nose against the window again. He saw crowds of people and newspaper photographers with big cameras that kept flashing and flashing.

"Oh, Mama! Look!" Kathleen cried. "I see Papa now!"

"Where? Where?" Teddy demanded. "I wanted to see him first."

"Oh, Teddy, it doesn't matter," his mother said. "We'll soon all be with him."

Just then, there was a knock on the compartment door. When Rosemary opened it, two uniformed British policemen, who were called bobbies, were standing there.

"Are you going to arrest us?" Teddy asked.

"Goodness, Teddy," Mrs. Kennedy said. "These men are here to escort us to your father."

"Yes, ma'am," one of the bobbies said. "There's quite a crowd here to welcome the Kennedy family to London, ma'am."

For the next several minutes, it was hard for Teddy to hear or see much of anything. He ended up squeezed between Jean and Eunice, who had each been given the task of holding one of his hands so he wouldn't get lost in the crowd.

Teddy had never heard anything like the shouts and the screams that assaulted them as the door to their coach was opened and they stepped out onto the platform.

"Why are they mad at us?" Teddy managed to shout up to Patricia.

"Oh, Teddy, they're not angry!" Patricia shouted back. "They're treating us like movie stars."

Teddy grinned. "Really?" he shouted.

Finally, everyone reached Joe Kennedy. Teddy grabbed at his father's greatcoat to get his attention. "Papa! Papa! I missed you so much!"

Joe Kennedy picked Teddy up, gave him a hug, and then held him up above the heads of everyone so the crowd could see his son.

Right away, a cheer went up, and people began shouting, "The prince! The prince! Let us see the prince!"

A beaming Joe Kennedy held Teddy up again to even louder cheers.

"Well, I guess they're not treating us like movie stars," Eunice said. "They're treating us like royalty."

"We are royalty," Joe Kennedy said. "*American* Royalty."

Slowly, the Kennedys made their way through the crowds that had packed the train station. At the doors to the street, they had to stop so the bobbies could clear those who were blocking the door.

"Back away now, please just back away!" one of the bobbies called through the partially opened door. "The Kennedy family needs to get to their automobile!"

Teddy kept ducking under the arms of his sisters, trying to get a better look, but just as quickly, one of them would pull him back into the center of their group.

Eunice leaned down close to his ear and whispered, "If you get lost in this crowd, Teddy, we'll never find you in time for sweets."

Finally, the crowd cleared a path from the door to the curb where Teddy saw a long black automobile waiting for them.

"What kind of automobile is that, Eunice?" Teddy asked.

"It's a Rolls-Royce, just like the one the Royal Family rides in," Kathleen told him. "We'll be using it while Papa is America's ambassador to the Court of St. James."

Inside, the automobile was so huge that the entire family could ride comfortably.

With the windows down, Teddy leaned out, still held tightly by Rosemary, and waved to the crowd that still lined the sidewalks around Waterloo Station.

When they finally reached normal traffic, which was still heavy, Teddy said, "Papa, where do we live?"

"The Ambassador's Residence, Teddy," Joe Kennedy said. "You'll like it, I think, because there are lots of places to explore."

In his head, Teddy tried to picture what the house would look like, but he wasn't prepared for what it actually was.

"Papa!" Teddy cried when the driver pulled

into the circle drive in front. "It's so big."

His father nodded and smiled. "Six stories. It used to belong to J. P. Morgan, the banker," he said, "but he donated it to our government."

As soon as he could get out of the automobile, Teddy started running toward the front entrance where some of the staff were standing to welcome the family.

"Hello," Teddy said to them. "I'm going to live here."

"You most certainly are, sir," an older lady said, "and we're all delighted."

"Wait up, Teddy!" Teddy turned. His older brother Bobby was running toward him.

When Bobby reached the front steps, he greeted the staff politely, then said, "Teddy, Papa told me that our house has lifts! Let's ride them up and down for a while."

"What are *lifts*?" Teddy asked.

"Elevators," Bobby replied.

For the next several minutes, Alfred, the

elevator operator, let Teddy and Bobby take turns closing the door and punching the buttons to the different floors. When all of the luggage had been placed on the first floor beside the elevator, though, they had to stop, but Alfred winked and said, "I'm here every day, so anytime you want to do this, just tell me."

"Thanks, Alfred," Teddy said. As they stepped off the elevator onto the floor where their rooms were, Teddy said, "I'm going to love it here!"

"Me too," Bobby said.

"I didn't think we'd *have* to go to school," Teddy said to Bobby two mornings later, as they headed toward the limousine that would take them to their day school on Sloane Street. "I thought we'd just be doing whatever we wanted to do."

"Oh, Teddy, of course we have to go to school," Bobby said. "We're going to live in London for a long time, and if we don't go to school, we'll be several grades behind when we go back home."

"I don't care," Teddy said.

Bobby rolled his eyes and climbed into the limousine.

Teddy was surprised to discover that he didn't dislike school that much after all. Most of his fellow classmates were British, so it took him a while to get used to the way they spoke, but they told him his American accent was hard to understand, too.

Not everything went well, though.

One evening, Teddy sought out his father in his office and said, "Papa, I want to talk to you about Cecil."

Joe Kennedy looked up from a letter he was reading and said, "Come here and sit on my lap, Teddy, and tell me about Cecil."

"He's in my class and he picks on me all the time," Teddy said.

"How does he pick on you, Teddy?" his father asked. "What is it that he does?"

"He's always waving the front page of a newspaper in front of my face," Teddy said, "and telling me that I'm not really a prince!"

"Well, to a lot of the British public, Teddy, you're *like* a prince, an *American* prince," Joe Kennedy said, "because the Royal Family only has princesses, Elizabeth and Margaret Rose, and the British are used to having princes around who will be future kings."

"Well, I still don't like it, Papa," Teddy said, "and I want your permission to fight him."

Joe Kennedy raised an eyebrow. "Oh, really? Well, I assume that you have given this a lot of thought and that you know very well what the ramifications of it could be."

"I've given it a lot of thought," Teddy said, "but I don't know what 'ramifications' means."

"It means that if you fight Cecil, you might win the fight," his father said, "but you might also get in trouble with the headmaster."

Teddy thought for a minute. "It would be worth it," he said.

The next day, when Cecil picked on Teddy again, Teddy slugged him. Cecil was surprised. So was the headmaster who had just appeared.

Teddy looked up at him. "It was worth it, sir," he said. "Now, I'm ready for my punishment."

"Mr. Kennedy, Sloane men are gentlemen," the Headmaster said, "but since I've just received a telephone message that your father's driver will pick you up in a few minutes to take you to Buckingham Palace, we'll not take this matter any further."

When the headmaster turned his back, Cecil made a face at Teddy, but when Teddy doubled up his fists and got into his boxing stance, Cecil fled.

Teddy stood by himself at the entrance to the school, feeling something he had never felt before. He wasn't exactly sure what it was, but he liked it, and he was going to tell

Bobby tonight to see if his brother knew.

Just then, the embassy Rolls-Royce pulled up in front of the school and Teddy ran out to get in.

On the ride to Buckingham Palace, Teddy questioned the driver about what he was going to do once he got there, but the driver would only say, "Your mother received a call from the palace about a hour ago, sir, telling her that the princesses requested your presence."

"Well," Teddy said, leaning back against the seat. "It's better than having to look at old Cecil all day."

"Yes, sir," the driver said.

Teddy had already been introduced to the princesses, when his father had presented his credentials as American ambassador to King George. In fact, both Elizabeth and Margaret Rose had told him they'd like for him to come to the palace for a visit sometime. When Teddy had mentioned that to Bobby, Bobby said, "I'm sure they're just being polite. I doubt if you'll ever get a personal invitation."

Well, you were wrong, Bobby, Teddy thought.

The driver stopped at an entrance guarded by a bobby who looked into the limousine and, upon seeing Teddy, said, "Well, sir, I'd recognize you anywhere. Your picture has been on the front page of several of our newspapers."

Teddy grinned. "People call me a prince," Teddy said, "but I'm not really . . ."

"Oh, sir, you are the *American* prince," the bobby said, "and today this is your palace."

He backed away with a bow and let the driver pull onto the grounds of the palace. In a few minutes, they arrived at a door where two footmen were waiting.

"They'll take you to the princesses," the driver said. "The palace will telephone the embassy when I need to call for you."

"Thanks," Teddy said.

Teddy followed the two footmen inside, down several corridors, and through several very large rooms until they reached a room with a door closed. One of the footmen knocked and then opened the door.

Inside, Princess Elizabeth and Princess Margaret Rose were surrounded by large balloons of different colors.

"Oh, Teddy, you came," Princess Margaret Rose said. "We wanted you to help us send messages around the world."

For the next several minutes, Teddy and the princesses wrote short messages on small pieces of heavy paper, added their addresses, and requested that whoever received the message please write back.

"We thought you'd like to write to people in America," Princess Elizabeth said. "We thought you might miss your country and that you'd like to receive letters from someone there."

Teddy had heard about people sending messages by balloons that traveled great distances. "Do you really think they'll reach my country?" Teddy asked.

"We hope so. We hope they reach people all around the world," Princess Elizabeth said. "We're telling everyone that we wish them all happiness and peace."

"We're adding 'peace' because our father doesn't want war," Princess Margaret Rose said. She looked at Teddy. "Does yours?"

Teddy shrugged. "I don't know," he said. "I'll ask him."

With help from various members of the staff, Teddy, Princess Elizabeth, and Princess Margaret Rose went out onto the grounds of the palace, behind a large garden, and began releasing the balloons one by one. They watched them soar high into the air. Finally, they could no longer see the last one.

Just then, one of the staff said, "Mr. Kennedy, your driver is here, sir, to take you home."

"Thank you so much for coming, Teddy," Princess Elizabeth said. She held out her hand and Teddy shook it.

"Will you promise to come back?" Princess Margaret Rose asked.

Teddy nodded. "I would like to very much," he said. "Will you show me your horses if I do?"

Princess Elizabeth grinned. "Oh, yes, I'd be happy to do that."

Over the next few weeks, Teddy's life in London was a whirlwind. When he and his nurse walked his dog, Sammy, on the sidewalks around the American Embassy or along the Thames Embankment, Londoners would stop and "ooh" and "aah" at him. During these walks, Teddy and his nurse would often stop to eat pastries at one of the nearby bakeries.

When the embassy hosted a Halloween party, Teddy dressed up like a Puritan and was the hit of the evening. Nobody seemed to mind, either, that he spent most of the time near the refreshment table snacking on delicious cakes and puddings.

One morning, Joseph Kennedy stopped

Teddy on his way out of the residence and said, "Sir Julian Huxley wants you to help him open a new pet corner in the London Zoo. I told him you would be happy to do that."

"Who's Sir Julian Huxley?" Teddy asked.

His father gave him a quick frown, but the frown quickly disappeared, and his father said, "He's an eminent biologist and educator, Teddy, a very important man, and I want you to remember that."

Once again, Teddy seemed to draw more attention than either Huxley or the animals, especially when he patted a zebra and the zebra bit him! Sir Huxley, to make up for the mishap, took Teddy to lunch, where he let him order everything he wanted from the menu.

One morning, a few days later, though, everything seemed to come crashing down.

Bobby started it with saying, "Teddy, have you looked in the mirror lately? You're getting fat!"

"No, I'm not," Teddy said.

"Oh, yes you are, little brother," Eunice said, as she passed him in the hallway. "You look like a butterball."

Suddenly, for the next two weeks, everyone in the family took an interest in Teddy's weight. They all had suggestions for helping him lose several pounds. They watched his diet, and they insisted that he exercise with them.

Then one day nobody said anything. Teddy wondered what had happened. When he asked Bobby about it, Bobby said, "We're busy with our own problems, little brother. Just be happy that no one expects you to do anything important when you grow up."

"How do you know that?" Teddy asked.

"I overheard Mama and Papa talking," Bobby replied.

Teddy thought for a minute, then he said, "All right, I'll be happy."

First Communion

One day in late August 1938, Teddy headed for his father's study to ask him if they could go horseback riding in the morning before he went to school. Just when he got to the half-open door, he was startled by his mother's shriek. He peeped through and saw his father kissing his mother and twirling her around and around.

"Oh, Joe, put me down!" his mother kept saying over and over.

"I shall do no such thing," his father said.

"Today I am a happy man, because Prime Minister Neville Chamberlain told me just a few minutes ago that Britain will do nothing if Hitler invades Czechoslovakia!"

Teddy decided he shouldn't interrupt his parents. He remembered when Princess Elizabeth had asked him if his father wanted peace and happiness instead of war. At the time, he really didn't know the answer, but of late his father had been speaking out more and more, on the radio and in newspaper interviews, about how Great Britain and the United States should not get involved in Germany's conquest of Europe and instead learn to live with the dictators on the continent.

Teddy had been happy to inform both of the princesses that his father was just like theirs. After Teddy chanced to overhear one embassy staff member say, "Of course old Joe is against the war, he doesn't want to lose his fortune," he asked his father what the person meant. His father said something about people not understanding what was really happening and then changed the subject, but Teddy noticed that he never saw that person at the embassy again.

One evening in March 1939, just after Teddy's seventh birthday, he sat down at the dinner table with the rest of the family, all prepared to discuss world events. His mother always posted news bulletins on a bulletin board in the kitchen, wherever they were living, and his father always tacked up a map of the world in the dining room, so he could explain not only what events were taking place in different countries but where those countries were. Often, Teddy either didn't know or couldn't remember what he had read or what he had heard his brothers and sisters talking about, but he was ready today to show everyone what he knew.

Instead, right after the first course had been served, Joe Kennedy said, "President

Roosevelt has named me his representative to the coronation of Pope Pius XII at the Vatican."

Jaws dropped and gasps were heard around the table, and then everyone applauded.

"Oh, Joe, Joe!" Mrs. Kennedy said, tears streaming down her face. "How great an honor to be there with the Holy Father for this historic occasion."

Teddy remembered the man who would be the next Pope. His mother said his name frequently: Eugenio Maria Giuseppe Giovanni Pacelli. He had even visited the Kennedy home during one of his tours of the United States as Cardinal Secretary of State.

"It truly is, Rose, it truly is," Joseph Kennedy said. "The conclave could not have chosen a better man at this time in our history. His diplomatic experience, especially with Germany, is needed."

• • •

There was a flurry of activity over the next several days, as the entire family, with the exception of Joe Jr. got ready to leave for Rome.

On March 12, the coronation took place at the Vatican. Teddy tried hard to understand the Latin words as the senior cardinal deacon said, "Receive the tiara adorned with three crowns and know that thou art Father of Princes and Kings, Ruler of the World, Vicar of Our Savior on earth, to Him be the honor and glory forever and ever."

When the crown was placed on Eugenio Maria Giuseppe Giovanni Pacelli's head, he became Pope Pius XII. The audience applauded and cheered.

The Pope then said prayers, which were followed by the Apostolic Blessing, and then once again the audience applauded and cheered.

When the ceremony was over, Teddy thought they would be leaving. He was getting sleepy, and he was getting hungry. But as the Kennedys stood up to leave, Mr. Kennedy said, "An even greater honor awaits us."

Teddy wanted to protest, but right at that moment a priest Teddy didn't recognize and two members of the Swiss Guard were suddenly beside their pew. The priest whispered in his father's ear, his father nodded and then said, "This way, everyone."

Within a few minutes, the Kennedy family was alone in a room with the Pope and three cardinals.

The Pope, who moments before had seemed to Teddy to be almost untouchable, was now greeting his family as though they had just dropped in on him at his house for a short visit. The Pope handed Teddy a rosary and said, "When you say your prayers, my son, remember today, and may the blessings of Almighty God, the Father, the Son, and the Holy Spirit be upon you and remain with you always."

As the Pope gave his brothers and sisters rosaries and pronounced the same blessing on them, Teddy was trying to make himself believe what had just happened. Two days later, he felt even more blessed, when he received his First Communion in the Pope's private chapel.

Outside, as they were heading toward the automobile that would drive them back to their hotel, his mother said, tears in her eyes, her voice breaking, "Teddy, you are the first young Catholic ever to receive that honor from His Holiness."

Once back in London, it didn't take long for things to return to normal. Teddy and Bobby were now going to school at Gibbs, which Teddy didn't find too different from Sloane. He had decided that there were "Cecils" everywhere. After a while, though, he got tired of being picked on, so he avoided anyone who seemed to be ready to make his life miserable.

Teddy still went horseback riding with his father before school, but his father was beginning to talk to him less and less about anything except how Great Britain and the United States should not go to war with Germany.

Teddy tried patiently to stay focused, but he was tired of hearing about it and had other things he wanted to discuss with his father.

Teddy himself hoped that the war wouldn't happen so that things would soon get back to normal. He not only didn't understand what was going on, but he wasn't really interested, and he was even beginning to wish his family would move back to the United States.

On September 1, things got even worse.

"Germany has invaded Poland, Teddy," Bobby whispered to him right before they left for school. "This means war."

"What will we do?" Teddy asked.

"Mama and Papa have been talking all

morning," Bobby said. "They're trying to decide."

As Teddy and Bobby headed downstairs to the dining room, Teddy thought he heard shouting. "Is that Papa?" he asked Bobby.

Bobby didn't say anything but his face looked grim. When they reached the bottom of the stairs, Teddy knew for sure it was his father and the shouting was coming from his study.

"Wake up, Mr. President! What is wrong with you and your administration?" Joe Kennedy was screaming. "This is the end of the world! Mark my word! You'll regret provoking Mr. Hitler! The United States should be his friend!"

Teddy looked at Bobby. "I've never heard Papa talk like that before," he whispered.

"I haven't either," Bobby said.

Teddy started toward the door of the study, but Bobby pulled him back.

"Don't go in there," Bobby said.

"I want to tell Papa I love him," Teddy said.

"Right now, he's not interested," Bobby said. "Leave him alone!"

Bobby left Teddy standing where he was. Teddy didn't know what to think now. How could his father not be interested in him just because a war had started? He was sure Bobby hadn't meant what he said.

But over the next few days, Teddy saw less and less of his father. He stayed at the embassy longer. He missed meals. When he was home, he stayed in his study and made it clear that he wanted to be alone.

As Teddy wandered through the building that had been his home for almost two years, he overheard the household staff whispering that his father's reputation was in ruins.

"Not only was he against the war," a driver said to a cook, "but he sold what stock he had in Czech companies and made an enormous profit from Hitler's invasion."

Even two of the nannies were talking about how members of the United States Congress were demanding that his father resign as ambassador and return home.

Teddy doubled up his fists and thought, *That's exactly what I want to do!*

Teddy got his wish. After Great Britain and France declared war on Germany because it had invaded Poland, the British began digging trenches, piling sandbags around buildings, distributing gas masks, and building air-raid shelters all around London.

"Joe, I'm taking the younger children back to America," Mrs. Kennedy told Mr. Kennedy a week later. "As our nation's ambassador, I know you have to remain here, but things are only going to get worse, so I think the rest of us should leave."

Mr. Kennedy nodded, but didn't look up from his plate, and Teddy felt a tear form in his left eye and begin to trickle down his cheek.

• • •

After a stress-filled voyage back across the Atlantic—stressful because of the fear of attack from German submarines—the Kennedy family arrived in New York. Earlier, Joseph Kennedy had bought a twenty-one-room redbrick Georgian mansion on six acres of land in the Bronxville area.

As soon as the driver pulled up to the front door, Teddy bounded out of the automobile, said a perfunctory hello to the staff, and began running all over the house, looking out windows, just to make sure there were no black curtains anywhere. In the days after the German invasion of Poland, blackout curtains had been hung all over their house in London and in the American embassy.

"Why?" Teddy had asked.

"So we can have the lights on without German bombers being able to see them," everyone told him.

Teddy couldn't imagine being anywhere

that planes were flying overhead, dropping bombs on people.

"I'm really happy here, Mama," Teddy said that evening at dinner.

"I am too, Teddy," his mother said.

"I miss Papa, though," Teddy added.

"I know you do," Rose Kennedy said. She looked up at him. "If you're finished eating, then go on upstairs and get ready for bed."

"Yes, Mama," Teddy said.

As he lay in bed that evening, waiting for sleep to come, Teddy wondered what it was going to be like being the only child at home now, with everyone else already away at university or at boarding school. He would miss his brothers and sisters, he knew, but now he wouldn't have to compete with anyone. He could just be himself. He liked that feeling.

• • •

Teddy was driven daily to Lawrence Park Country Day School. It was so much better than the two schools he had attended in London.

"I just feel more at home here than I did there," Teddy said. "They speak English, even though it's hard to understand sometimes, but I never really liked any of my classmates."

"Well, we all heard you were considered a prince over there," one of his new classmates said.

Teddy nodded. "But none of the fellows at either one of my schools liked that," he said.

Teddy had hoped now that he was the only child in the house, that he and his mother would do things together, but Rose Kennedy had taken a suite at the Plaza Hotel in Manhattan, where she started staying for longer periods of time.

Teddy telephoned her once to ask, "May

I come on Friday and stay with you for the weekend, Mama?"

His mother said, "No, Teddy, darling, I've already made plans for those days, and I really can't break them. I'll talk to you soon."

Teddy's disappointment lasted only a few minutes. He received a telephone call shortly afterward from the mother of one of his new classmates inviting him to stay at their house for the weekend.

"I'll be happy to," Teddy told her.

"Shouldn't you ask your mother first if it's all right?" the woman said.

"Oh, no, ma'am, Mother lets me decide these things for myself," Teddy told her.

When Rose Kennedy did return to the house in Bronxville, she seemed more distant than she ever had before. Teddy would tell her about what was happening to him in school and what he and his friends were doing, but she only talked to him about the latest fashions and the trips she planned to take soon.

One morning at breakfast in early December, Rose Kennedy put down her coffee cup and said, "We're all getting together at our house in Palm Beach for Christmas, Teddy. And that includes your father."

"Oh, Mama, that's wonderful," Teddy said.

Mrs. Kennedy smiled. "I thought you'd think so, dear," she said.

When the holidays finally arrived, though, the happiness Teddy had been looking forward to was somewhat muted. Although he loved being with his brothers and sisters again, playing on the beach, swimming in the Atlantic, and sailing along the coast, when he overheard his mother and father talking about him in his father's study, he went from being happy to being sad in a matter of seconds.

"I simply cannot and will not rear Teddy by myself, Joe—not while you're sulking about in England," his mother said. "So I've decided he will be sent off to boarding school just like his brothers and sisters."

Parachutes over Nazi Germany

In March of 1940, just after Teddy's eighth birthday, he received a letter from his father, who was still in London. For a while, after they had returned to the United States from England, the letters had arrived with relative frequency, but after Thanksgiving of the previous year, they had dropped off.

"Mama! Mama!" Teddy cried as he raced

through the house. "Let me read Papa's letter to you!"

When he couldn't find his mother anywhere, he asked one of the cooks where she was.

The cook gave him a surprised look and said, "She's at confession, sir." She pointed to the clock on the wall. "She goes every day at this time."

Teddy took the letter out onto the back porch and sat down in a wicker chair. He carefully undid the flap, so as not to damage the stamps.

As Teddy began reading what his father had written, he felt tears welling up in his eyes, and at that moment, he wanted so very much to be sitting on his father's lap, as he read the comics or told him about all the things that were happening around the world. Teddy didn't want to be reading about how lonely and frustrated his father felt and how much he missed his family.

Teddy looked up. "Papa, please come home," he said. "I miss you so much. I don't want you to be sad."

Teddy turned back to the letter and its graphic descriptions of the nightly bombing raids on London, but he was glad to learn that there was a nearby shelter. He knew his father would be safe until he could come back home.

That night, Teddy put the letter under his pillow along with the other letters he had received from his father and went to sleep thinking about happier times at Hyannis Port or Palm Beach or even here in Bronxville.

As the winter days turned into spring ones, Teddy brightened somewhat, thinking about the upcoming move to their summer home at Hyannis Port, Massachusetts. Life moved at a slower pace there, since everything was less formal, and there was the sun and the sand and the inviting waters of Nantucket Sound for swimming and yachting. At the back of his mind, though, Teddy feared that this summer might be different.

He still had nightmares about leaving home to attend boarding school. He couldn't imagine ever doing that. From time to time, though, he would overhear his mother talking on the telephone to ask people "school" questions. She never seemed happy with their answers, and he hoped that she never would be.

A few weeks earlier, his brother Jack's book, *Why England Slept*, had been published to rave reviews, but Teddy had also overheard Bobby talking to Jean about how their oldest brother, Joe Jr., was very unhappy about it.

They wouldn't tell him why when he asked, though.

"What's the book about, Jack?" Teddy asked when he talked to his brother in a rare telephone conversation a couple of days later. "Would I enjoy reading it?"

"It might be a bit dry for your tastes, Teddy,"

Jack told him. "It's about how Great Britain failed to take steps to prevent World War II."

"Oh," Teddy said. "I guess you're right."

"But Mother has a copy of the book, I'm sure," Jack said, "so if you want to take a look at it, just borrow hers."

"Okay," Teddy said. He hesitated for a moment. "I wish everyone in the family had a copy, Jack. Could you make sure they do, and could you can sign your name in it too. Joe Jr., Kathleen, Eunice, Patri—"

"I have to run, Teddy, but I'm looking forward to seeing you in Hyannis Port this summer," Jack said, interrupting the list. "It'll be like it always was."

As it turned out, Teddy didn't even have to ask anyone else why Joe Jr. didn't like Jack's book. One of his cousins volunteered the answer during a short visit to the Bronxville house with his parents.

"Joe Jr. is angry with Jack for writing such

a popular book, because now everyone thinks that Jack looks more knowledgeable about the war than Joe does," the cousin said. "Joe is also angry with your father for helping to get the book published and for doing so much to promote it afterward."

"Joe wouldn't get mad about that," Teddy insisted.

"Oh, yes, he would," the cousin said. "My father told me that Joe, being the oldest, expects to be the most important son in the family, and now it seems that Jack is." The cousin looked around. "I wouldn't want to be around them at Hyannis Port this summer," he added menacingly.

After that conversation, Teddy had begun to dread what would happen between Jack and Joe Jr. once everyone returned to Hyannis Port for the summer of 1940. He was pleasantly surprised when everyone seemed relaxed and interested only in having a good time.

Almost right away, long distance race competitions were held that not only included his brothers and sisters, but also friends they had made from previous summers. Although Teddy ran as hard as he could in all of the races he entered—because everyone was expected to compete at their highest possible level—he didn't win any of the trophies that were awarded. He didn't tell anyone, but he didn't care, for he was enjoying just being there.

One afternoon, a boy named Ralph, who was staying with family friends two compounds down from the Kennedy's, pulled him aside and said, "Do you know how to jump out of an airplane with a parachute?"

Teddy shook his head. "I've never had to do that," he said.

"Well, I know, and you need to know it, too," Ralph said. "If you're ever in an airplane over Germany and those Nazis shoot it down, you'll die if you don't jump out."

For just a minute, Teddy pictured himself in a disabled airplane, over Hamburg or Berlin or Frankfurt, as it plummeted rapidly toward the buildings below. He looked Ralph in the eye. "Can you teach me how?"

Ralph looked around to see if anybody was watching them. He nodded. "You'll have to get a couple of sheets, though," he said. "The housekeeper where I'm staying wouldn't let me have any."

"Do we need anything else?" Teddy asked.

Ralph shook his head. "Nope," he said. "I have plenty of cord."

Teddy managed to slip out of his house with two white sheets and make his way back to the family compound where Ralph was staying.

Ralph met him at the edge of the property and said, "This way. If the housekeeper sees us, she'll think I took the sheets after all."

There were enough trees and shrubs on the property that Teddy and Ralph were hidden until they reached a garage some distance away from the main house.

"Nobody parks inside this building," Ralph said, "so we should be able to practice our jumps without anyone telling us to stop."

"Why would they tell us to stop?" Teddy asked. "After all, what we're doing may save our lives one of these days."

"Well, you know that, and I know that," Ralph said, "but my parents are always saying things like 'Don't do that, Ralph! You're going to break a leg!'"

It suddenly occurred to Teddy that Ralph's parents might be right, but there was no way he was going to back out now, not after thinking all afternoon that this was the only way he'd be able to save himself if he were ever flying over Germany and the Nazis shot him down.

Inside the garage, Ralph found a ladder, and, with Teddy's help, they moved it to the far side of the building. Then they sat down and tied a pieces of cord to each of the four corners of their sheets.

"I wish we had real parachutes inside packs," Ralph said, "so we could pull the rip cord, like we'll have to do when we're being shot down by those Nazis over Germany."

"Yeah, me too," Teddy said.

"Come on," Ralph said. "It's time to bail out of our plane."

Together, Teddy and Ralph climbed to the top of the garage. Teddy was suddenly surprised at how high off the ground they were.

"We'll jump off the other side," Ralph said. "There's a lot of sand over there, and it'll break our fall."

Teddy thought that was the first sensible thing Ralph had said all day.

"You jump first," Ralph said. "I'm the pilot, so I have to jump last."

"Why can't I be the pilot?" Teddy asked.

"Because you haven't been to pilot school like I have," Ralph replied.

Teddy knew there was no sense in continuing this discussion, because he knew Ralph would have answers to all of his questions.

"Okay," Teddy said. He grabbed the four ends of the cords, put the sheet behind his head, stood at the edge of the garage, and jumped.

For just a minute, he felt the air being trapped by the sheet. But he landed in the sand with a thud, before his "parachute" could fully inflate. Right away, he saw a few stars, but they quickly disappeared, and he was on the ground in Berlin, with the Nazis rushing toward him.

Teddy looked up at Ralph standing at the edge of the garage. "Jump! Jump! The plane's going to crash if you don't," he cried. "The Nazis know where we are, and they're going to capture us!"

But Ralph wasn't paying any attention. He was looking at something behind Teddy. That

something turned out to be the housekeeper.

"Those had better not be my sheets," the housekeeper said.

"No, ma'am," Teddy said. "They're my mother's."

"Well, you fly on home, and I don't want to see you jumping off this garage again," the housekeeper said. She looked up at Ralph. "Come down from there and follow me into the house, young man!"

Ralph did was he was told.

Teddy watched him follow the housekeeper into the house. A couple of days later, when Teddy asked where Ralph was, he was told that Ralph's visit was over and that he had returned home to Delaware.

On Sundays, the Kennedy family always went to Mass at St. Francis Xavier Church on South Street in Hyannis Port. It had been their church since Joe had bought the house in the 1920s. The summer wasn't halfway over, though, before one morning at breakfast, Mrs. Kennedy said, "Don't make any plans for this morning, children, because we're going to Mass."

Teddy gave his mother a strange look. "But Mama, it's Wednesday, not Sunday," he said. "Have you forgotten?"

"Of course I haven't forgotten, Teddy," Mrs. Kennedy said. "I've decided it's time this family realizes that Sunday is not the only time for going to church."

Teddy opened his mouth to complain, but Jean kicked him under the table.

"Ouch!" Teddy cried.

For the rest of the summer, in addition to Sunday Mass, the family went to church on at least two other days during the week— and sometimes three. Teddy still complained but always only to his brothers and sisters. He soon learned that they were more upset about the fact that their mother's life now centered almost solely on the church than about taking up what few summer days they had left by going to church during the week.

"I've known nuns who went to church less," Bobby muttered one morning.

Eunice quickly crossed herself and said, "If you don't go to confession and confess what you just said, Bobby, well, I'll . . . I'll . . ."

"Oh, I shall," Bobby muttered.

As if the additional masses weren't enough, Mrs. Kennedy soon began taking the children on religious retreats at different places on Cape Cod.

"I had planned for us all to go sailing this weekend," Bobby said. "Now, that's out of the question." He looked at Patricia. "I didn't think I'd ever wish the summer would be over so I could return to school."

Teddy thought he saw in the faces of his brothers and sisters that they wished the same thing.

Boarding School

In October of that year, 1940, Teddy's father returned to the United States and asked President Roosevelt to relieve him of his ambassadorship to Great Britain. But Roosevelt was so occupied with his presidential campaign that he ignored Joe Sr.'s request.

After Roosevelt was elected for a third term on November 6, he signaled that he would accept Joe Sr.'s resignation, so on December 1, Teddy father's wrote a letter to Roosevelt officially resigning as America's ambassador to the Court of St. James.

To Teddy, this meant that his father would no longer be an ocean away from him, so the Christmas of 1940 was a relatively happy time for Teddy. Almost every room of the Bronxville house was decorated for the holiday season.

On several occasions, Teddy accompanied his mother into Manhattan to shop for presents for members of the family. Teddy thought there was no place on earth as colorful as New York at Christmastime.

For the most part, when everyone finally arrived for the holidays, they tried to leave the usual Kennedy competitiveness outside in the cold—except for the few occasions when someone challenged someone else to a snowball fight.

The meals never seemed so glorious to Teddy, nor the tables so full, and no one said anything when he kept coming back for second and third helpings.

Then it was suddenly over, and, as everyone began to leave, to return to where they had been before the holidays, Teddy felt as though the house had started to close in on him. In a way, he was looking forward to being the center of attention again.

But right before Bobby left for Portsmouth Priory, the school he attended in Rhode Island run by the strict Benedictine monks, he said, "I'll see you soon, Teddy," and then he gave his brother a wink.

Before Teddy could recover enough to ask Bobby what he meant, his brother was already in the automobile that would take him to the train station for the short trip to Rhode Island.

Teddy didn't have to wait long to find out. Right after New Year's Day, his mother invited him into her room and said, "Although you're really too young for Portsmouth Priory, Teddy, I've talked to some of my dear friends, and I've been able to enroll you there."

Teddy wanted to protest loudly, but he remembered the whispered conversation between his parents in Florida, so the words wouldn't come out of his mouth except in stammers. The look on his mother's face made him stop trying to say anything.

Within a week, Teddy was being driven by Marks, the family chauffeur, to Rhode Island, his bags full of new clothes because his old clothes no longer fit him very well.

"What happened to my clothes?" Teddy had asked his nanny as he was helping her pack his suitcases.

"They had too much Christmas," his nanny replied.

Teddy knew she meant that *he* had had too much Christmas *food*.

Portsmouth Priory School had been founded by a group of Benedictine monks in 1926 to offer a British upper class form of education to boys. The school emphasized the classics—and athletics after classes.

When Teddy and Marks arrived, Teddy looked at the campus on the shores of Narragansett Bay and thought it was incredibly beautiful, but he also remembered some of the stories that Bobby had told him—and his mother's parting words. "The mission of Portsmouth Priory School, Teddy," she had said, "is to emphasize the importance of reverence for God and man, to learn respect for education and order, and to share the experience of communal living."

After meeting with the headmaster, Marks helped Teddy carry his luggage to his room. There were six beds and six lockers. Five boys, all larger than he was, stared at Teddy as he and Marks unpacked the suitcases.

When they finished, Teddy looked into

Marks' eyes, hoping that Marks would understand that what he really wanted to do was get back into the automobile, drive back to Bronxville, and hide in his room forever.

Please say you'll do that, Marks! Teddy pleaded silently.

Instead, Marks put his hand on Teddy's shoulder and said, in a soft voice, "You have to do this, son. You have to prove that you're as good as the rest of them."

With that, Marks turned and left the room. Teddy watched Marks's back disappear, but he didn't turn around for several minutes. When he finally did, a fist hit him right in the face.

For Teddy, Portsmouth Priory School was one failure after another. When he was in his room, his roommates pushed him and punched him until he cowered in a corner and begged them to stop. When they stopped the physical assaults, the verbal assaults began.

His extra weight made him the least physically fit boy in the school, and no one let him forget it. After a while, Teddy lost count of the different names he was called. When Teddy was in class, it was even worse. He had never before thought he was stupid, but after he had attended the first meeting in each of his subjects he began to believe his teachers and fellow students when they all said he was the dumbest person they had ever known.

On the playing fields, balls and sticks of one kind or another always found him as the target.

When Teddy complained to Bobby about what was happening to him, Bobby told him he had to fend for himself, because that was what Kennedy men did.

At night, as Teddy listened to the snores and breathing patterns of the five other boys in his room, he tried to understand how his life had gone from being the American prince in London to being assaulted several times daily by a group of teenagers in Rhode Island.

As the end of that term at Portsmouth Priory neared, Teddy was able to sustain himself with the knowledge that he would soon return home to Bronxville where he would be safe with his parents and his brothers and sisters, but a rare letter from Jack sent him running to find Bobby.

For once, Bobby was in his room, alone, lying prone on his bed, a book only inches from his face.

"May I interrupt you, Bobby?" Teddy asked tentatively.

Without changing his position, Bobby said, "I don't particularly like the poems of Gaius Valerius Catullus, Teddy, even in the original Latin, so yes, please do."

Teddy handed Bobby his letter from Jack. Bobby unfolded it, placed the letter against the open book, and started reading. In a few minutes, he sat up. "What's the problem?" he asked.

"Mama is on a trip to South America, and no one knows when she'll return," Teddy said, "and Papa is upset about a lot of things and is selling the house in Bronxville."

"That's right," Bobby said.

"Aren't you unhappy?" Teddy asked.

"Well, I'm not unhappy that Mama is traveling, because it's good for her to do things she was never able to do when we were all younger," Bobby said, "but I'll miss the house in Bronxville, because there are a lot of good memories associated with it."

"But what about the part where Papa is upset?" Teddy asked.

Bobby stood up. "Teddy, Papa is Papa, and nothing will ever change him," he said. "He believes what he believes, and right now he believes that the important people in this country don't think much of him because of his views on the war."

"What are we going to do, Bobby?" Teddy asked.

"We'll do what the Kennedys have always done," Bobby said. "We'll take on any challenge and any challenger, and we'll be the first ones to cross the finish line."

When Teddy left Bobby's room, he felt more alone than ever. His mother was in South America. His home had been sold. His father was thinking only about what Americans were saying about him.

And his smart and talented brothers and sisters were focused on their own individual lives.

When the end of the term finally arrived, Marks came to drive Teddy to the house at Hyannis Port. All the way there, Marks tried to get Teddy to talk about one thing or another, but Teddy mostly grunted and looked out the window.

• • •

That first week, friends and family came and went—all except for Rosemary. When Teddy finally asked about her, his mother got up and left the room without a word.

"Rosemary wasn't like the rest of us, Teddy," his father said after a few minute of strained silence. "It's best that she live where there are people who understand her and can take care of her better than we can." Then he stood up himself and started toward the stairs, but two steps up, he turned and added, "Please don't ever again mention Rosemary's name in this house."

Teddy decided then that it would be best if he didn't expect anything in particular to happen that summer. He would enjoy who was there, and he wouldn't miss anyone who wasn't.

When Joe Jr. arrived, though, Teddy felt a surge of happiness that he hadn't expected. Joe Jr. had always been the next best thing to his father. When Joe Jr. asked Teddy if he wanted to take a walk along the beach, Teddy immediately accepted.

With the incoming waves washing over their bare feet, they laughed and joked about things they had done in the past, but then Joe Jr.'s face lost all traces of its laugh lines and he said, "Teddy, I want to be this country's first Catholic president."

Teddy gasped, then he hugged Joe Jr.'s waist. "Oh, Joe! I'd vote for you!" he said. "I'll even campaign for you."

Joe Jr. looked surprised. "I didn't know you were so interested in politics," he said.

"Didn't anyone tell you?" Teddy asked incredulously. "Last year, at my school in Bronxville, Westbrook Pegler II and I debated—"

"Is he related to that columnist Pegler?" Joe asked, interrupting.

"He's a nephew," Teddy said. "Anyway, I spoke for Roosevelt, and Pegler spoke for Wendell Willkie, the Republican."

"You must have done a good job," Joe Jr.

said, "because Roosevelt won the election."

Teddy grinned. "But when the school had a straw vote, Willie won," he said.

Joe Jr. returned Teddy's grin. "I still want you on my campaign team," he said.

By the middle of the summer, Teddy had decided that he never wanted to return to Portsmouth Priory School. He wasn't exactly sure how he'd manage this, short of running away from home, but he began a concerted effort to convince everyone that it would be a terrible thing. As bad as things had been for him, he tried to make them sound even worse.

But Teddy's father only told him that he was extremely disappointed that Teddy had been whining, and that he should be more like British boys his age who had to deal with German bombs pounding London on a daily basis.

Teddy was devastated.

For a couple of days afterward, Teddy tried to make himself believe that his father was right, that returning to Portsmouth Priory School would be what a *real* Kennedy man would do. But then one day, everything changed. Joey Gargan, an older cousin who had never before been around the family that much, arrived. The two became constant companions, and began a friendship that would last a lifetime and help Teddy begin to make his own decisions.

"I can't go back there, Joey," Teddy said. "I hated that school and everyone there, except for Bobby, of course."

"Teddy, part of your duty to your family is to understand yourself well enough to succeed on your own merits," Joey said. "You can't be someone you're not."

So Teddy didn't budge on his decision. His mother told him that she wouldn't press the issue and that in the fall Teddy would be going to the private Riverdale Country School in New York City, because even the Benedictine monks thought it would be best if Teddy didn't return to Portsmouth.

In his head, Teddy fantasized that Riverdale would be the exact opposite of Portsmouth Priory. In his new school, he would be the smartest and the most athletic student there.

As it turned out, it couldn't have been worse. From the first day, his attendance was irregular at best. Just being in a school setting again caused him so much stress that his health was affected. Added to that were the constant comments from people around him, both students and adults, about his father. They told him that he was a disgrace because of his antiwar and almost pro-Hitler sentiments.

One morning, Teddy awakened and could hardly breathe. The family doctor who came to examine him said, "It's pneumonia." Later, the pneumonia turned into whooping cough.

On December 7, the Japanese bombed Pearl Harbor, Hawaii, and suddenly the United States was at war. A few days later, war was declared on Germany.

By the time the Christmas holidays arrived, though, Teddy was up, moving around, and feeling almost normal. The comings and goings of the family brightened his spirits immensely, although most of the talk was about the war.

At the beginning of the next year, the Kennedys left for Florida to spend the winter there. When they arrived, Rose tried to enroll Teddy in a private school in Palm Beach, but the headmaster, after looking at Teddy's Portsmouth Priory and Riverdale records said, "I'm afraid your son is simply not prepared for the fourth grade, Mrs. Kennedy. We'll simply have to put him at a lower level where he might possibly succeed."

On the way back to their house, no one said anything to overweight, underachieving, and insecure Teddy.

The Best Friend Ever

In January 1942, newspaper columnist Walter Winchell wrote about Jack's friendship with Danish journalist Inga Marie Arvad, whom the FBI suspected was a Nazi spy.

"That gossipmonger!" Joe Kennedy shouted, throwing down the newspaper. He turned to Teddy. "What I'm about to do next is something you need to understand," he said.

"Yes, sir," Teddy told him.

Teddy followed his father into his study and closed the door behind them.

While Teddy sat in a chair next to his father's desk, Joe Kennedy asked the operator to connect him with J. Edgar Hoover, the director of the FBI, in Washington, D.C. "And tell him it's Joe Kennedy," Joe said. "He'll take my call."

When Mr. Hoover came on the line, Teddy's father exchanged a few pleasantries with Hoover, then he said, "I want you to make sure there will be no criminal charges against Jack. In return, I'll be happy to give you the information you want about the Communist activities of people I know."

After Teddy's father hung up from speaking with Hoover, he asked the operator to connect him with James Forrestal, the undersecretary of the Navy, also in Washington, D.C. "Tell him it's Joe Kennedy. We're friends. He'll take my call."

When Mr. Forrestal came on the line, Joe Kennedy said, "There is no way I'll allow Jack to be dishonorably discharged from the

Navy, Jim, so I want you to transfer him to torpedo boat school so he can then be sent to a patrol torpedo boat squadron in the South Pacific."

When his father hung up the telephone the second time, he looked at Teddy for a few minutes, then he stood up and said, "That's the way Kennedy men do business, son, and I never want you to forget that."

Within days, Jack was assigned to the Navy shipyard at Charleston, South Carolina and soon afterward graduated from Motor Torpedo Boat Squadron Training Center as a skipper.

After that, Teddy seldom saw his father or his mother. Joe Kennedy was occupied with his own activities, and Rose Kennedy had returned to South America by herself to visit shrines to the Blessed Virgin Mary.

Over the next few months, Teddy tried

to make the best of his life, as Marks drove him back and forth between a school in Palm Beach, where he was doing fourth grade work, and the Graham-Eckes Academy, a few miles away, where he was doing fifth grade work. At both schools, he was barely passing.

On May 6, Joe Jr. received his naval wings after graduating from flight school. Joe Sr. took Teddy with him to the ceremony.

On the way home, Teddy's father said, "The Kennedy men are achievers, son. They must always be better than other men."

That summer of 1942, Teddy felt especially lonely. He wanted to be up in Hyannis Port, but his mother had decided that not only would he stay in Florida, but he also would attend special summer tutoring sessions at both schools in the hopes that he would eventually be able to reach the grade level he should be in for his age.

With fewer classmates around, and with knowing that those who were there had the same problems as he did, the summer didn't create as much anxiety in Teddy as he had expected. And Saturdays he had to himself, spending most of the day walking along the beach, looking for shells.

When regular classes started again in the fall at both schools, Teddy's anxiousness returned, and with it a decline in his performance, both academically and athletically.

His self-esteem, always very low, fell even lower when, one day in early March 1943, just after his eleventh birthday, he saw a letter his mother was writing to family members who were in Massachusetts and read that she was happy that at least now Teddy was making less of a fool of himself than usual.

Finally, the spring terms at both schools ended, with Teddy still either failing or barely passing most of his classes. He knew his performance was not up to Kennedy standards, but now all he could think of was returning to Hyannis Port and an entire summer on Cape Cod.

"Joey!" Teddy shouted when Teddy saw his cousin getting out of an automobile that had just pulled up in front of the Kennedy Compound. "You finally got here."

"We had a flat tire," Joey said. "It took a while to get it fixed."

Teddy and Joey helped the driver carry Joey's suitcases into the house and up to Teddy's room.

"I asked them to put another bed in here so we can talk as late as we want to," Teddy said.

"I was hoping you'd do that," Joey said.

"We've got two years to catch up on," Teddy said. "There are a lot of things happening."

"You can say that again," Joey agreed. "I've got a lot of stuff to tell you, too."

• • •

Although Teddy knew how much he liked Joey, it took almost all of that summer for him to verbalize it.

"You never make fun of me, Joey," Teddy said, "and you never laugh at me."

"Why would I do that?" Joey asked.

Teddy shrugged. "You're everything I think a friend should be," he added.

"Why are you so surprised?" Joey said. "I thought you already knew that."

"Sometimes, I really don't know what I know," Teddy said, looking out his window at the nearby shore.

On August 2, Teddy and Joey were just leaving the house when they saw Teddy's father's jump off a horse he'd taken out for a morning ride, hand the reins to his trainer, and start running toward the house.

"I wonder what's wrong with Papa," Teddy said. From the look on his father's face, he knew it wasn't something good.

Joe Sr. rushed past both boys without saying anything to them. Teddy looked at Joey and they went back into the house. Teddy's father was in his study, on the telephone, shouting, "Tell me everything! I want to know everything! Is Jack still alive?"

Teddy felt the blood drain from his face. He didn't think he could bear it if Jack had been killed.

It seemed as though it took forever but, finally, Joe Sr. hung up the receiver. By now, most of the rest of the family, as well as some of the staff, had gathered outside the door of the study.

"There's been a terrible accident," Teddy's father began, "but Jack's alive."

To Teddy, that was all that mattered. Even when he learned that two of his brother's men on *PT 109* had been killed when a Japanese destroyer rammed the boat just off the Solomon Islands in the South Pacific, he still could only think about the family not having to mourn Jack.

In the newspaper the next day, Jean showed him and Joey a huge article on the front page. "They were stranded in the middle of the Pacific, Teddy, but Jack managed to save the rest of his crew."

"They should give him a lot of medals," Joey said. "He's a real hero!"

Teddy couldn't believe everyone was talking about his brother. It sounded more like a character in one of the exciting movie serials he and Joey had seen that summer at a theater in Hyannis Port.

Even when Teddy overheard his father saying to someone on the telephone, "There's no way it was Jack's fault, so I'd better not see that in print!" it made no impression on him whatsoever. His brother was a hero, and he would always be a hero.

The United States government felt the same. Jack was awarded medals from both the Navy and the Marine Corps.

•   •   •

A few days later, while Joey was talking to Jean about the movie they were all going to watch that night, Teddy saw his father sitting alone in his study, with the lights off, his face in his hands.

"What's wrong, Papa?" Teddy asked.

Joe Sr. looked up, and for a minute, Teddy thought his father didn't recognize who he was. Then he said, "Come in, Teddy. We haven't talked in a while, son."

Teddy entered his father's study, sat down on a side chair, put his elbows on the edge of the desk, and rested his chin in his hands. "I always love talking to you, Papa," he said. "You always tell me the most interesting things."

"Well, here's something new," his father said. "I just talked to Joe on a transatlantic call, Teddy, and he told me he's joining a new aerial combat unit in England that will be flying missions over Germany."

"Does he know how to use a parachute?" Teddy asked anxiously.

His father gave him a strange look. "Why would you ask such a question, son?" he said.

Teddy started to tell him all about how he and Ralph had jumped off the garage of a nearby compound when they were pretending that their airplane had been shot down by the Nazis, but instead, he said, "I just want him to be safe."

"So do I," Joe Sr. said. He looked away, adding, "Why did Jack and that Japanese destroyer have to collide? Why did this have to happen now?"

Teddy didn't have to ask why his father was saying that. He knew. Whenever something happened to his brother Jack that made headlines around the world, Joe Jr. felt pressured to do something that would make even bigger headlines.

That summer, Teddy began making Sunday trips by himself into Boston for lunch and a visit with his Grampa Fitzgerald, his mother's father, whom everyone called Honey Fitz. Teddy loved these trips, because it was quite clear from the moment his grandfather saw him that he considered Teddy special.

One particular Sunday, they decided to have lunch in the dining room of the hotel where Mr. Fitzgerald lived.

"Not only is the food good here, Teddy," his grandfather said, "but I like to see people I've known for a long time, so I can wish them happy birthday or tell them how sorry I am that one of their loved ones died."

All during lunch, Teddy watched in amazement as his grandfather would take a bite of food, then acknowledge someone passing by their table with a "Happy birthday, David. I know it was two days ago, but I'm just seeing you now, friend"; "I'm sorry about the death of your niece, Anna. She was such a lovely young lady"; and "I'm glad to see you up and about, Philip, after that bout of pneumonia, so you take care of yourself, especially when it gets colder."

"How do you know all of this, Grampa?" Teddy asked.

His grandfather grinned, then he pulled a handful of newspaper clippings out of his pocket. "I read a lot," he said.

Teddy had seen the newspaper clippings hanging out of his grandfather's pockets on several occasions, but it had never occurred to him to ask why they were there. What really amazed him, though, was that it was the first time anyone had ever shown him any real practical use for reading.

In the fall of 1943, Teddy enrolled at The Fessenden School in West Newton, Massachusetts, for what would be fifth, sixth, and seventh grade work.

Bobby was in nearby Milton Academy, and had promised Teddy in Hyannis Port that

he would telephone him more frequently this year.

Bobby kept his word. Although they would talk about what they had done the previous summer and about their future plans, Bobby seemed mostly interested in Teddy's studies.

"I don't like any of my classes, and I'm still being bullied," Teddy said with as much exasperation in his voice as possible. "So what else is new?"

"Well, since you're still whining about it, I guess nothing is new," Bobby would always say, "but don't expect me to help you either with your studies or with figuring out how to get along with people."

"Thanks a lot, Bobby," Teddy said. "Was there anything else you wanted?"

Bobby wouldn't take the bait. Instead, he said, "I need to get away this weekend, so I thought I'd pick you up and then we'll spend the weekend at the Hyannis Port house."

"It's all boarded up for the winter, Bobby," Teddy said.

"I know, and that's what'll make it fun," Bobby assured him. "We'll cook our own food, we'll sleep on cots, and it'll be one of the best times you've ever had."

As it turned out, it really was.

The War Comes Home to Hyannis Port

The winter excursions with Bobby to the boarded up house in Hyannis Port came to an abrupt end when, just a couple of months into the school year, Teddy was taken out of the sixth grade at Fessenden and enrolled in the sixth grade at the Graham-Eckes school in Palm Beach.

"After long considerations, Teddy, your father and I have decided that this is what's best for you," his mother told him, once they had arrived in Florida. "You'll be living at home, so your progress in your subjects can be closely monitored."

Teddy wasn't exactly sure what had happened, whether it was the wonderful winter weekends with Bobby, where being a Kennedy man had begun to seem more appealing to him, or if it was simply that he was tired of knowing that everyone in the family had given up expecting anything from him.

Whatever the reason, it really didn't matter, because when Teddy left the house on the first day he was to attend classes, he made a vow that he was going to prove once and for all to his family that there was still hope for him.

Teddy's parents were true to their word. They talked to him at dinner every evening about what he had done in each class that day and checked on him several times later to make sure his homework for the next day had been completed.

"We're proud of you, Teddy. You're beginning to show some of that true Kennedy tenacity," his mother told him one morning before he left for school. "It seems as though we've found the right answer to this problem after all."

Teddy smiled and said, "I guess it really was there all along, Mama, but just needed a little prodding to show up."

His mother returned his smile. "I guess, dear," she said. "It's been an interesting experience for both your father and me."

By the middle of the spring term in 1944, twelve-year-old Teddy was receiving Bs in English and math and As in history and writing. During this time, he also won his first election. He was voted vice president of the sixth grade.

By April, though, Teddy's success was once again overshadowed by another member of the family: his sister, Kathleen. He came home one afternoon to find his mother screaming on the telephone, "How could she possibly marry him? He's a Protestant!"

The loud protestations coming from his mother lasted more than an hour, until with a strangled sob, she slammed down the telephone and, without another word, climbed the stairs to her bedroom and locked herself inside.

It was only later that he learned from Jean that Kathleen was engaged to William Cavendish, the Marquess of Hartington and the future Duke of Devonshire, a wealthy member of the British aristocracy.

"Why is Mama so upset?" Teddy asked.

"She's worried that the Pope will excommunicate Kathleen," Jean explained, "and she knows for certain that the children of British royalty can only be reared as Protestants."

Teddy tried to remain positive about all of

the good things that were happening to him in school, but suddenly every member of the family's attention was focused either on Kathleen or on their own lives. Once again, Teddy seemed to be an afterthought.

On May 6, Kathleen married William Cavendish and became the future Duchess of Devonshire. The event caused Rose Kennedy to have a nervous breakdown.

The Kennedys returned to Hyannis Port for the summer of 1944. Jack had come to Hyannis Port to convalesce from his injuries in the PT boat disaster, so Rose wanted to continue her own convalescence there, as well, surrounded by more of her family.

Teddy was glad to leave Florida, too, because his grades had once again started to drop, and he was fast losing interest in proving himself to his family.

That summer, Teddy and Jack reconnected as brothers.

One evening, Jack held up a book and said, "Let me read something to you, Teddy. It's Stephen Vincent Benét's *John Brown's Body*."

"What's it about?" Teddy asked.

"This country's Civil War," Jack replied. "It's one of the most widely read American poems, and it's a wonderful retelling of that very important event in American history."

Teddy didn't really like poetry, but he didn't say anything, and he lay on the floor next to Jack, who was stretched out on a sofa, and let Jack's voice fill the room.

> *"Army of the Potomac, advancing army,*
> *Alloy of a dozen disparate, alien states,*
> *City-boy, farm-hand, bounty-man*
>   *first volunteer,*
> *Old regular . . ."*

For the next hour, Teddy listened to Jack's voice as it brought alive the words he was reading. It created in him a sensation he had never felt before. Jack was his brother, yet he also seemed to belong to another world, and it sent shivers through Teddy, realizing that this could be what everyone meant when they said the Kennedys were very special people.

Suddenly, Jack stopped and said, "My back is beginning to hurt, Teddy, so I think I need to get up and move around some. We'll finish this later, if that's all right."

"Sure, Jack, thanks," Teddy said. "I really like it." He watched as his brother grimaced. "Is there anything I can do for you?"

"Well, you can make this pain go away," Jack said as he pushed himself off the sofa.

"If I could, I would, Jack," Teddy said.

Now standing, Jack said, "I know you would, little brother, I know you would."

"I really do want you to read to me again, Jack," Teddy said, now standing up himself. "I wasn't just saying I liked it, I really did."

●　　●　　●

True to his word, over the next few weeks, Jack read to Teddy from books about famous political lives, such as Edmund Burke and Daniel Webster. Teddy was disappointed that he didn't enjoy them as much as *John Brown's Body*, so he was glad when everyone seemed to drift back into their old habits of being consumed only by things that directly affected them.

Teddy's mother still spent most of her days in her own bedroom, but she had begun to leave the house for a few hours on Sunday to attend Mass, after weeks of having one of the local parish priests come to the Kennedy house to say a special Mass.

Joey Gargan arrived in Hyannis Port about this time, too, having spent the first part of the summer in Maine.

"I ate lobsters three times a day," Joey told Teddy. "I used to like them, but now I can't stand the sight of them."

"I don't think I could ever get enough lobster to eat," Teddy told him. "I think they're delicious, especially with garlic butter."

"Stop!" Joey shouted. "You're making me sick!"

It wasn't long before Teddy and Joey picked up where they had left off the previous summer. Teddy could talk to Joey about anything, and Joey would just listen. If Teddy asked him what he thought, Joey would tell him, and it was always something positive.

On August 12, Teddy and Joey were just coming back from the beach when they noticed two Catholic priests walking up to the front door of the Kennedy house. Teddy knew that different Catholic charities often came by, asking for donations, but he sensed this time that was not the case.

"I think we need to hurry," Teddy whispered to Joey.

They quickened their pace so they were

just behind both of the men as Eunice invited them inside. Teddy could hear Patricia's voice calling her mother and father.

Once everyone had gathered in the parlor, one priest sat down next to Teddy's mother, and the other priest next to Teddy's father.

"There is no easy way to break this news to you, Mr. and Mrs. Kennedy, and to the rest of your family," the first priest said, "but your son Joseph Kennedy Jr. died in a plane crash. He was flying over the English Channel on a secret mission, and—"

"No, not Joe Jr.!" Teddy's father cried. "Not my boy, not him!"

The rest of the day and night was a blur to Teddy. As the rest of his immediate family arrived, along with extended family and friends, Teddy seemed to get lost in the crowd. The cook fed him supper before he went on up to his room and lay down on his

124

bed. Somehow, he felt that this was all his fault. He should have shown Joe Jr. how to make a parachute the way Ralph had shown him. Now, his brother was dead because of that mistake.

For days, people came and went, but Teddy stayed mostly in his room. Occasionally, Bobby would drop in to see how he was doing, but then he would leave.

The house was filled with the sounds of the operas of Richard Wagner coming from their father's bedroom. When one opera ended, another one started, and the music lasted all through the day and through most of the night.

On September 9, the Kennedy family received word that Kathleen's husband, William Cavendish, was killed in battle against the Germans.

"Oh, Kit, poor Kit," Patricia said. "She's

already a widow after only being married for four months."

That fall of 1944, Teddy returned to Fessenden School as a seventh grader, but now he was all consumed with anger, and he went out of his way to make sure he broke the rules, was rude to anyone who spoke to him, and smashed anything breakable he saw. After several visits to the headmaster's office, Teddy was told that everyone at Fessenden understood the awful tragedies that the Kennedy family had suffered, but that his behavior would not be tolerated much longer.

Two days later, just as Teddy had made the decision to destroy everything in his room, he opened his door to a knock and found Bobby standing there.

"May I come in?" Bobby asked.

"What are you doing here?" Teddy asked. "Did you get kicked out of Harvard?"

Bobby grinned. "No, I just wanted to check

on you," he said. He came into the room and sat down in the one chair that wasn't stacked with either clothes or books. "I know how hard you took Joe Jr.'s death."

"I'm not the only one, Bobby," Teddy said.

"No, you're not, but I know what a difficult time Mama and Papa are having trying to cope with it," Bobby said, "so I doubt if they've even telephoned or written you since you've been here."

"They haven't," Teddy said.

"Teddy, being a Kennedy is both a blessing and a curse, and I've told you this many times," Bobby said, "but everyone else has gone their separate ways, fending for themselves emotionally, and expecting the rest of the family to do the same."

"I'm not like the rest of the family, Bobby," Teddy said. Tears had formed in his eyes and were about to spill over. "I'm not as smart, and I'm not as talented."

Bobby took Teddy in his arms and hugged

him tightly for several minutes; then he said, "It may take a little longer, Teddy, and there may be more sorrow in your life, but you will find yourself one of these days, and you will like what you see."

Teddy pulled apart and looked Bobby in the eye. "Do you really believe that?" he asked.

"I believe it with all my heart, Teddy," Bobby said, "and I'm going to be there when it happens."

I'm a Kennedy
Man Too!

Bobby was true to his word, and life for Teddy at Fessenden began to get better and better. Although no one said anything to him, Teddy could see in their eyes that their thoughts went from "Should I punch you?" to "Are you *really* Teddy Kennedy?"

One day, about a week after Bobby's visit, Teddy knocked on the office door of Fessenden's football coach, Jory McGuire.

"I want to be on the team, Coach," Teddy said hesitantly.

Coach McGuire looked him up and down and said, "Well, you're big enough, Kennedy, but I'm not sure you have the discipline."

"I won't disappoint you, sir," Teddy said, "if you'll just give me a chance."

Teddy watched as Coach McGuire seemed to be considering every reason why he should say no. Finally, his mouth set grimly, he said, "All right, we'll give it a go, because I need a bigger center to keep our opponents from getting to the quarterback, but your reputation precedes you, Kennedy, and I won't tolerate any nonsense from you."

"I understand, Coach," Teddy said. "I won't let you down."

Teddy kept his word. He was used to playing football, especially at Hyannis Port with his brothers, who gave him no slack whatsoever, but being on a *real* team with a *real* schedule was different. Teddy soon learned the true meaning of "teamwork." Although he initially played center, easily keeping opposing teams from even getting near the quarterback, as the season progressed, Coach McGuire moved him around until he finally decided that right tackle would be where Kennedy could really contribute to each game.

His academic grades slowly began to rise, too, and he even made the honor roll. Teddy began to experience a happiness and contentment in his life that he had never known before.

Teddy wasn't sure how Bobby managed to get away so often from his studies at Harvard, but he frequently sat in the bleachers during football practice and always seemed to show up just when Teddy had questions about a book he was reading or a paper he was writing.

Still, there were times when Teddy's desire to rebel in some way clouded his judgment, especially when he was with a close friend like Danny Burns, who seemed made out of the same cloth.

"Mr. Moore keeps a jar of candy on the desk in his office, Teddy," Danny said one evening. "I asked him for a piece once, when I went to him with a problem I was having with sourcing my geography paper, but he said he only had enough to last him until he went back to Switzerland this summer."

"Mmmm, Swiss chocolate, my favorite," Teddy said.

"Mine too," Danny said.

That was all it took. With a few tools that could pick any lock, Teddy and Danny opened the door to Mr. Moore's office and helped themselves to several pieces of the candy.

Just as they turned to leave, though, Mr. Moore flipped on the lights. "Well, well, well," he said. "Fancy meeting you here."

"We were just hungry, that's all, Mr. Moore," Danny said, "and so we—"

"Burns, for this little episode, I'm going to deduct some points from your next geography paper," Mr. Moore said, "and Kennedy, since I don't have you in one of my classes, thank goodness, your punishment will be to sleep in your bathtub tonight."

"Yes, sir," Teddy said. He thought that was a strange punishment, but he wasn't going to argue, because he knew Mr. Moore could have him expelled. "I'll do that, sir."

"And Kennedy," Mr. Moore added, "I've noticed you haven't been in the Fessenden station wagon that takes our Catholic students to Mass every Sunday, so I suggest that this next Sunday you set your alarm to make sure you go." He cleared his throat. "I'm sure you have a lot of things to confess."

Teddy almost regretted the end of the spring term, but not enough to keep him from thinking about how wonderful it was going to be at Hyannis Port that summer.

So he was disappointed when nobody really seemed interested in hearing how well he had done that past year at Fessenden School, and how he really believed that he was finally showing the world he was a Kennedy man, too.

Teddy's mother seemed to be attending Mass more and more frequently, and his father, still grieving for Joe Jr., but still carrying the dream that one of his sons would become President of the United States, had now turned to Jack to fulfill these political aspirations. Jack, now out of the military, was working as a journalist reporting on the new United Nations in San Francisco and on the British Parliament.

Joey Gargan spent several weekends with Teddy that summer, and they tried to recapture some of their past glory days, but in the end that consisted mostly of "talking" about all of the things they had done in summers past and wondering what the future really held for them.

As the end of August neared, Teddy began thinking about the coming football season at Fessenden School and the league title that the team hoped to win this year, but one morning at breakfast, all those hopes were dashed.

"I'm enrolling you at Cranwell for the eighth grade, Teddy," his mother said.

Teddy took a deep breath, while he tried to control his rising anger, then he slowly let it out. He had heard about Cranwell Preparatory School. It was in the town of Lenox in the wilderness of western Massachusetts, almost at the border with the state of New York. A friend had once described it as something out of a Charles Dickens novel.

"Why, Mama?" Teddy finally said. "You know how much I like Fessenden, and I was looking forward to playing football there again this season. We think we'll win the league."

"Teddy, it's important to attend a Catholic school in order to build your character and to shore up and strengthen your religious underpinnings," his mother said, "and the Jesuit fathers have dedicated their lives to doing just this."

With that, his mother returned to her coffee and her newspaper, and Teddy knew that the discussion was over.

On the drive to Cranwell that September, Teddy kept saying to Marks, "There are no people around here. There's no civilization around here. Why would anyone build a school in the middle of nowhere?"

"It wasn't built as a school, Teddy; it used to be a private residence," Marks told him, "and I've heard it looks just like one of those really large royal estates in Great Britain."

"I'm going to be a character in a novel by Dickens this year, Marks," Teddy said sarcastically. "That should be a lot of fun."

Although around every corner and in every passageway Teddy expected to see Oliver

Twist or David Copperfield or Ebenezer Scrooge—or any of the other characters from Dickens' stories and novels, life at Cranwell itself didn't turn out to be as awful as he had thought it would be. But the remoteness of the area meant no one came to visit him.

"They probably can't find it," Teddy complained to his roommate.

"Or maybe they don't want to," his roommate said.

Teddy looked at him. "I was talking about *my* family, not *yours.*"

"Sure, Kennedy, sure," the roommate said as he turned the page of the book of poetry he was reading.

That evening, Teddy called Bobby at Harvard. "Teddy, I don't think I can make it out there," his brother told him. "I've doubled up on my classes this term because I have some other plans for the spring."

An hour later, when Teddy finally reached his mother, she said, "No, Teddy, dear, I don't think I can come out there anytime soon, because of the distance, but I promise I'll send you postcards from Argentina."

Teddy's father wasn't home. He had gone to Chicago to buy the Merchandise Mart, the largest privately owned building in the world. His mother didn't know in which hotel he was staying.

With his football experience at Fessenden School, Teddy was sure he would be the star player on Cranwell's team, but he was surprised to see how very good the other players were. Some of them had even been contacted by coaches from major universities.

Teddy was welcomed to the team, because of his size, but he soon realized that everyone else was faster than he was. At one practice, Teddy saw two priests in their robes standing along the sidelines watching their drills.

"Kennedy, you're too slow," one of the

priests shouted. He was grinning. "I can out-run you in my robes."

"Oh, really?" Teddy shouted back.

"Really!" the priest said.

Now, everyone had stopped practice to watch the exchange.

"Okay," Teddy said. "Let's just find out."

Teddy and the priest lined up at the fifty yard line.

The coach said, "The first one in the south end zone is the winner." He blew his whistle.

For the first twenty yards, Teddy was ahead, but the priest, pacing himself, passed Teddy and reached the goal line first.

In public, Teddy was a good sport about losing the race, but in private he began to question his athletic ability if he couldn't even outrun a priest who was twice his age.

In February, Bobby called Teddy to tell him he would soon begin a tour of duty aboard the *USS Joseph P. Kennedy, Jr.*, a destroyer

that had been launched on July 30, 1945. Teddy would miss the brother he had begun to count on more and more, but he was proud to know one brother would be serving on a ship named for another.

At the beginning of June, just before the school year at Cranwell ended, fourteen-year-old Teddy learned that, in the fall, he would be going to Milton Academy, in Milton, Massachusetts, the same high school Bobby had attended. Now, Teddy could relax and enjoy the upcoming summer at Hyannis Port.

Milton Academy

When fourteen-year-old Teddy entered the ninth grade at Milton Academy, just south of Boston, he had finally started to believe that his life really would have meaning.

Bobby had preceded him at the school and had paved the way for him. Certainly, Teddy would have to succeed on his own, but he believed from the very beginning that he would never again feel alone and isolated.

Earlier that year, in April, Jack had announced that he would run for Massachusetts's Eleventh Congressional District seat, which had been left vacant by James Michael Curley, who wanted to once again run for mayor of Boston. This was the same Congressional seat that Teddy's grandfather John "Honey Fitz" Fitzgerald had held almost a half century earlier. Now that Jack had won the primary, there was almost no question that Democratic Boston would vote for him. That meant Jack would represent the district for the next two years. This only served to boost Teddy's morale and self-assurance as one of the Kennedy men.

When Teddy moved into Forbes House, the second-largest residence at Milton, he was assigned to the same room Bobby had stayed in. Teddy saw that as another sign that all was well with his life.

"Kennedy, we're going to raid Wolcott tonight," his roommate said. "We're going to get the Forbes flag back. Are you with us?"

Teddy nodded. "You can count on me," he said. "Bobby is still angry that the flag was stolen again during the last week he was here."

Around ten o'clock that night, five Forbes men positioned themselves outside the service entrance to Wolcott.

"We know where the flag is," another roommate whispered. "We have someone on the inside."

"Are you telling me that one of the Wolcott men is a traitor?" Teddy asked.

His roommate grinned. "No, it's one of the plumbers," he said. "He's angry about how a couple of the Wolcott men talked to him when their toilets overflowed, so he thought this would be a perfect way to get even with them. He even loaned me a key to this door."

Teddy nodded. "There's a lesson in that, men," he said. "Be nice to everyone, especially the plumbers."

144

The raid went off without a hitch. In fact, when the Forbes men were discussing it later, they were all somewhat disappointed that they didn't encounter any resistance from the Wolcott men.

The next day, though, several of the Forbes men reported seeing shocked looks on the faces of some of the Wolcott men as they walked by Forbes on their way to classes and saw the Forbes flag flying.

"They'll never figure out what happened," Teddy predicted. "It'll be the biggest mystery on campus all year."

"We're going to the Totem Pole tonight, Kennedy," Johnny Vincent, a Forbes man who lived two doors down from him, said. "Why don't you come along?"

"What's the Totem Pole?" Teddy asked.

"It's a dance hall for teenagers in downtown Milton," Vincent said. "A lot of girls from around the area come in on a Saturday night." He grinned. "They all like Milton men."

"Well, since I'm a 'Milton man,'" Teddy said, "I guess I'd better go check this out."

The Totem Pole turned out to be a round building with tiers of couches and twinkling lights that reflected off rotating mirrored balls hanging from the ceiling. Teddy couldn't believe how crowded it was. It turned out it was the largest dance hall for teenagers in the state of Massachusetts. It soon became one of Teddy's favorite places to be on a Saturday night.

On Sundays, though, Teddy made sure he attended services at a nearby Catholic church. It wasn't long before he was even asked to help serve Mass.

Although academics were stressed at Milton Academy, and Milton men were expected to do very well in all of their subjects, the school also made it clear that to be well-rounded, a Milton man should participate in as many extracurricular activities as possible. Teddy took up the challenge.

He became a formidable member of the Debate Team. Several of his co-debaters who were upperclassmen asked him how he already knew so many ways to win arguments.

"I'm a Kennedy," Teddy told them. "This is what we do for fun during meals."

In the Glee Club, his voice soared in the solos he was asked to sing.

But it was as a member of the Boogies that Teddy really found his niche. This group thrived on pulling stunts, both on campus and in the town of Milton.

"It's underwear tonight, men," Tad Hathaway told the group gathered in his room. "We'll leave at midnight."

So at eleven-thirty, five members of the Boogies slipped out of Forbes, all wearing only their underwear, and headed down the street.

"We are we going tonight?" Teddy asked.

"There's a movie theater about four blocks from here, and the last show gets out at midnight," Tad said. "We'll hide in the shadows until several people have come out, and then we'll run by them, turn the corner, and head down the alley instead of the next street, in case the Milton police happen to be patrolling the area."

"I guess they frown on this," Teddy said.

"You're very perceptive, Kennedy," Tad said. "You have a bright future ahead of you."

Almost exactly at midnight, people started exiting the theater, and on Tad's command, the five Forbes men started running down the sidewalk, Teddy bringing up the rear, whooping and hollering, passing startled movie patrons, some of whom started screaming, thinking they were being attacked.

It all went off without a hitch, and everyone made it back to Forbes without being spotted.

148

The next day, Teddy saw a small article about the stunt on the back page of the Milton newspaper. He tore it out and put it inside a book, thinking he might show it to his children one day.

Teddy met with even more success as a member of Milton's football team. He was no longer overweight, having worked really hard in the last few months to get his weight down and to turn what was left to muscle. He was now six feet tall, muscular, and fearless when it came to tackling opponents.

Just after his fifteenth birthday, in February 1947, Teddy was asked by the parents of one of his friends what he thought about Milton as a school. Without hesitation, he said, "It's a secure and friendly place. It's *home*."

Politics and
Family Secrets

In May of 1947, as fifteen-year-old Teddy's first year at Milton was coming to a close, he went to Hyannis Port to celebrate his brother Jack's thirtieth birthday with the rest of the family. Teddy was looking forward to seeing everyone. He wanted to tell them how well things were going at Milton. He also wanted to hear from Jack what it meant to be a member of the United States Congress.

When Teddy finally arrived, there were the obligatory hugs and kisses and handshakes, but then everyone returned to what they had been doing before Teddy got there.

At first, Teddy was disappointed that it wasn't just his immediate family there for the celebration—a lot of Jack's friends who were helping him realize his and his father's political ambitions had been invited too—but Teddy knew this was the way politics worked, so he would find a way to deal with it.

Finally, Teddy was able to corner Jack just as he was coming out of one of the bathrooms at the rear of the house.

"So how are you doing, Congressman?" Teddy asked with a grin.

Jack returned Teddy's grin. "I think I was meant to do this, Teddy, because it all feels right," he said. "Although I must say I didn't think I'd be so opposed to some of Truman's ideas." Jack shook his head. "I think that man needs to go back to Missouri, Teddy.

He just doesn't fit the Washington mold."

"That's what I hear a lot of my friends at Milton saying too, Jack," Teddy said. "They think you should be president."

"Well, we're talking about that, although it's not to be repeated, at least not anytime soon," Jack said. "But things are going to have to change in the Democratic Party first, because some of us, myself included, are just not connecting with a lot of our fellow politicians."

"What's the problem?" Teddy asked.

"I'd say it's mostly the Congressmen from the Old South," Jack replied. "Right now, they pretty much have a stranglehold on us, and it's hard to get anything through their thick skulls."

Teddy laughed. "You'll be able to charm them, if anyone can," he said.

"Oh, Jack! You're needed!"

Teddy looked around to see who was calling his brother, but he didn't recognize the man.

"I'm coming," Jack called to him. He turned back to Teddy. "You keep up the good work at Milton, then you'll do well at Harvard, and then Bobby and you can join me in Washington." He gave Teddy another big grin. "We Kennedy men are going to change the world, Brother!"

A few minutes later, everyone was called to lunch. Although the fit was tight, there were enough seats for every member of the family and all of the guests at the large round table. The menu was extraordinary, Teddy thought, but he had promised himself that he wouldn't gain back any of the pounds he had shed for football, so he took small portions of a few of his favorites but turned away the desserts.

After everyone had finished, Joe Kennedy stood and proposed a toast to Jack, the son who he knew would fulfill the father's dreams of glory for the Kennedy family.

To Teddy, this seemed to be a toast that

should have been made with only immediate family members present, but, as he looked around the table at the faces of the guests, he saw nothing that would betray anything but the same desire. He found it almost incredible to believe, and even a little disconcerting that he was now a member of a family that had just tripled in size. He was sure that the definition of what it meant to be a Kennedy man had taken on broader and more complex meanings, forcing him to work even harder for the smallest recognition.

"Now, my dear family, our dear friends," Joe Kennedy said, "I want us to go around the table, so each of you will have the opportunity to express in your own words how you feel at this special moment."

At each stop, the person would stand, express in different words what had already been said, praising Jack's past successes and wishing him many more successes in the future.

When it was Teddy's turn, he could not think of any words that would be different from what had already been said, so he stood, raised his glass, and said, "I want to propose a toast to Joe Jr., the brother who is not here." With that, he took a sip from his wineglass, but then he realized that he was the only one drinking, that everyone else was staring at him in disbelief.

Later, upstairs, Teddy saw Jean and said, "What did I do wrong?"

Jean gave her brother a quick peck on the cheek. "It's a family taboo, Teddy, to speak openly of one of our tragedies in public."

All the way back to Milton, Teddy felt terrible about the toast and wondered over and over why he could never seem to do anything right.

Back at Milton, though, with just a few remaining weeks of the spring term, Teddy easily slipped back into his comfortable routine.

While he might never reach the success of the rest of his family, Teddy was happy with the success he had achieved in his first year at Milton. Additionally, he had already made the conscious decision that, rather than looking at his family in negative terms, from now on, he would spend his summers at Hyannis Port focusing on what it meant to be a Kennedy.

At Hyannis Port that summer of 1947, Teddy's disastrous toast was never mentioned. Teddy and Joey Gargan spent hours talking about whatever came to mind, but when the time came to leave Cape Cod, to return to school, they realized they were only halfway through with their list of things they had planned to tell each other.

When Teddy returned to Milton Academy that fall of 1947, he continued working as hard as he could to improve his grades. He won even more debates on the Debate Team.

To the team member who had told him the

year before that he ought to go into politics, he said, "I have decided to take your advice about running for political office. When I decide when and where, I'll let you know, and you can either be my campaign manager or my largest contributor."

"I'm going to remember that, Kennedy," the boy said, "so I hope you're not just saying it."

"Oh, I never say anything I don't mean," Teddy told him.

In September of that year, though, the Kennedy family received word that Jack had been diagnosed with Addison's disease, a rare endocrine disorder, by Sir Daniel Davis at The London Clinic. At a family meeting at Hyannis Port, Joe Kennedy swore his family and the members of Kennedy's political team to absolute secrecy. "I shall not have this destroy the political career of my second son," he shouted to everyone. "This news will not see the light of day!"

● ● ●

Back at Milton, Teddy was named co-captain of the football team. The attendance at the games was up, especially among the girls of Milton and surrounding towns, and that seemed to bring out even more athletic ability among the players.

Teddy also took every opportunity to have fun, and he soon added to his reputation of being one of the first people you invited to any party.

In May of 1948, though, sixteen-year-old Teddy's life was once again rocked—by the death of his sister Kathleen in a plane crash over France. Kathleen's husband, William Cavendish, had been killed four years earlier fighting the Germans, making Kathleen a widow after only four months of marriage. Upon learning the news, Teddy rushed to Hyannis Port immediately to help console the rest of the family.

Teddy returned to finish out the term at Milton, still somewhat numb from Kathleen's death, but he had kept up so well with his subjects during the year that his final grades didn't suffer, so he could return to Hyannis Port for the summer with the knowledge that he now knew he could suffer tragedy and still focus on whatever obligations he had.

In June, Teddy joined the family in Cambridge, Massachusetts, to witness Bobby's graduation from Harvard College. Instead of attending Harvard Law School, though, Bobby decided to study for the bar at the University of Virginia.

Try as he might, though, once Teddy was back at Hyannis Port for the summer, he couldn't shake off a darkness that now seemed to surround him. Several times, he tried to explain it to Joey Gargan, but the words would never come together in the right order so they would make sense—until one evening toward the end of July.

"I have eight brothers and sisters, Joey," Teddy said, "and in my sixteen years three of them have already disappeared from my life: Joe Jr., Rosemary, and Kathleen."

When Joey didn't say anything, Teddy added, "Why has my family had to endure such tragedies, Joey? Why were we chosen? Do you have an answer for that?"

Joey shook his head. "I don't know, Teddy," he said, "I just don't know."

In the fall of 1948, Teddy returned to Milton for his junior year. The routine there was now so ingrained in him that it had become second nature, and that only increased his comfort level. But when he learned during a telephone call from Jean that Jack was still suffering the consequences of Addison's disease, which caused him extreme fatigue and was affecting his immune system, it created an anxiety in him that made it difficult to stay focused some of the time.

On several recent occasions, Jack had jokingly wondered just how much longer he would be around. To Teddy, there was nothing funny about this. He couldn't bear to think what would happen to his father if Jack succumbed to his illness.

When Jack was reelected to Congress that fall by an overwhelming majority, though, Teddy realized that what some had begun to call "the Kennedy magic" had worked again. The family bar was getting higher and higher, Teddy knew, but unlike in the past, when that seemed to push him down, it now buoyed him, and he saw it as a challenge he planned to meet.

With Jack now back in Congress and with Bobby finishing his law degree at the University of Virginia, Teddy threw himself even more into making sure he would leave his own mark at Milton Academy.

The fall of 1948 turned into the spring of 1949, and Teddy only occasionally stayed at Hyannis Port that summer, preferring to look around Cambridge and the campus of Harvard.

When seventeen-year-old Teddy returned to Milton Academy in the fall of 1949, he had thought he'd be able to savor his last year of high school, but the year seemed to fly by, and before he knew it, he was walking across the graduation platform, with most of his family in attendance, to receive his diploma. After it was handed to him and he had started toward the steps that would lead him back to where he had been sitting with the other graduates, he happened to look up, and, for just a moment, he thought he saw Joe Jr., Kathleen, and Rosemary, all smiling at him.

Harvard, Europe, and Law School

In the fall of 1950, Teddy entered Harvard College, following in Jack and Bobby's footsteps. He easily made the freshman football team, where he played both offensive and defensive end.

At the beginning of the spring semester of 1951, Teddy moved into Winthrop House, where most of Harvard's male athletes lived.

Teddy's grades during that first year were

marginal at best, and he was concerned about maintaining his eligibility for athletics, so he could join the varsity football team. The course he was most worried about was Spanish. At Teddy's request, a friend of his who was very good in Spanish agreed to take the final exam for him. The deception was quickly discovered by Harvard administrators, and both Teddy and his friend were expelled from the school. But, as was standard procedure at Harvard in such cases, they were told that in a year, preferably two, they could apply for readmission, provided they had demonstrated good behavior during that time.

In June 1951, Teddy enlisted in the United States Army, a traditional punishment for the wayward sons of upper-class families. After he completed basic training at Fort Dix, New Jersey, Teddy requested that he be assigned to the United States Army Intelligence Center at Fort Holabird, Maryland.

After only a few weeks at Fort Holabird,

though, Teddy was dropped from the course, without any formal explanation given, and was sent to the Military Police Corps at Fort Gordon, Georgia, for training to become an MP. He successfully completed the course, and in June 1952 he received orders to report to SHAPE (Supreme Headquarters Allied Powers Europe) part of NATO (North Atlantic Treaty Organization), in Paris to be a member of the Honor Guard. It was a choice assignment, since he could have been deployed to Korea, where the Korean War was raging, but Joe Sr. had used his political connections in Washington to make sure that didn't happen.

In his off duty time while he was assigned to SHAPE, Teddy traveled extensively around Europe. He even climbed the Matterhorn in Switzerland.

In March 1953, Teddy received his discharge from the Army as a private first class.

That summer, Teddy reentered Harvard

College and vowed to improve his study habits.

There was no way he was going to completely ignore his social life, though, so he joined the Hasty Pudding Club, one of the oldest collegiate social clubs in the United States, known for its elaborate "theme" parties. Jack had been a member when he was at Harvard, and so were Presidents John Quincy Adams, Theodore Roosevelt, and Franklin Delano Roosevelt. Teddy also joined the Pi Eta fraternity.

Although Teddy was on athletic probation for his sophomore year at Harvard, he was able to return to the football team during his junior year, but only as a second-string end. Still, he barely missed earning a varsity letter.

During his senior year at Harvard, Teddy became a starting end on the varsity team. He spent hours and hours on the practice field working with the coaches to perfect his blocking and tackling. It paid off. With those

honed skills, along with his height of over six feet and his weight of two hundred pounds, he was a formidable opponent. Although Yale won the 1955 game against Harvard, 21–7, Teddy was the one who made Harvard's only score, catching a pass in the end zone for a touchdown.

His performance on the field was good enough to attract the attention of professional football coaches, especially Lisle Blackbourn, head coach of the Green Bay Packers. When Blackbourn asked Teddy if he would be interested in playing professionally, Teddy told him that he wouldn't, that he had plans to attend law school so he could go into politics.

At Harvard's 1956 graduation exercises, Teddy received his BA in history and government. That fall, just as Bobby had done, he enrolled in the University of Virginia School of Law.

In early October 1957, the Kennedy family gathered at Manhattanville College, a prestigious Catholic woman's college in Purchase, New York, to dedicate a sports complex building in the memory of Kathleen Kennedy. Teddy delivered the dedication speech. Afterward, Jean, who was herself a graduate of the college, introduced the family to a friend, Virginia Joan Bennett. Teddy and Joan, as she was called, were immediately taken with each other and soon began a long-distance courtship. Teddy, who was in his second year of law school at the University of Virginia, telephoned Joan every night. As often as they could, they went on frequent—and heavily chaperoned—dates. Joan spent time with Teddy in Hyannis Port with his family, and Teddy spent time with Joan's family.

When Teddy proposed marriage to Joan at the end of summer in 1958, Joan accepted.

Marriage, Family, and a Presidential Assassination

Right after Teddy's proposal, though, Joan began to grow nervous about marrying someone she suddenly realized she didn't know very well.

Joan had led a relatively sheltered life. Although she had won several beauty pageants and had worked as a model, the world of politics was completely alien to her. In fact, right after she had first met Teddy, she confided to friends that she had never really heard much about the Kennedy family. But not only was marriage to Joan what Teddy wanted, it was also what Teddy's father wanted, and Joe Kennedy would not be put off, so he insisted that the wedding take place as soon as possible. Teddy and Joan were married at St. Joseph's Church in Bronxville, New York, by Francis Cardinal Spellman, on November 29, 1958.

The Kennedys were now rapidly emerging as a political force in the country. Everything seemed to be going according to Joe Kennedy's master plan.

It hadn't been lost on Jack that his little brother had charisma that connected with ordinary voters, so he asked Teddy to manage his 1958 Senate reelection campaign. Teddy, almost heady now with the realization that he really did have personal qualities that could be put to good use for the family, campaigned tirelessly, and was one of the primary reasons for Jack's record-setting victory margin that made Washington pundits start talking about his brother's possible presidential aspirations. As happy as Jack and Teddy were, Joe Kennedy was even happier.

Teddy graduated from the University of Virginia School of Law in 1959 and was admitted to the Massachusetts Bar a few months later. Then he and Joan took a belated honeymoon to South America.

On February 27, 1960, Teddy and Joan became parents of Kara Anne.

Teddy was soon put to work campaigning in the Western states for Jack's presidential bid. He even learned to fly. During the Democratic primary campaign, Teddy flew all around the western part of the United States, meeting convention delegates and showing that he was one of them by participating in rodeo events and in ski jumping. All his hard work paid off.

Jack won Wisconsin, the first contest primary. The time Teddy spent in Wyoming was rewarded by Jack's receiving a unanimous vote from that state's delegates at the 1960 Democratic Convention in Los Angeles. That was more than enough delegates to make him the Democratic candidate for the 1960 presidential election.

On November 8, by a very narrow margin, Jack defeated Richard M. Nixon, the Republican candidate and Dwight Eisenhower's vice president, to become the thirty-fifth President of the United States—and the first Roman Catholic.

After his election, Jack vacated his Massachusetts Senate seat. Teddy made no secret of the fact that he wanted to be the one to fill Jack's vacant Senate seat, but he wouldn't be eligible until he turned thirty, which would be on February 22, 1962. Although both Jack and Bobby were against

Teddy's plan, their father overruled them, and Jack, as president-elect, appointed family friend Ben Smith to fill out his term, in effect keeping the seat open for Teddy.

While he waited for his thirtieth birthday, Teddy took a position in February 1961 as an assistant district attorney in Suffolk County, Massachusetts, earning a yearly salary of one dollar. It was during this time that he became a strong voice against any kind of criminal activity. He also began speaking to area clubs and organizations to keep his face before the public.

Teddy and Joan's second child, Edward Moore Kennedy Jr., was born on September 26, 1961.

In the 1962 special election for Jack's former Senate seat, Teddy faced a Democratic Party primary challenge from Edward J. McCormack Jr., who was the attorney general of the state. McCormack had strong support from many of the state's liberals, who all thought Teddy was too young and inexperienced.

During the campaign, McCormack's supporters made sure Massachusetts voters knew about Teddy's suspension from Harvard for cheating on his Spanish exam. McCormack himself also asked over and over at each campaign stop if those in attendance thought that Teddy was one Kennedy too many, since his brother Jack was the president and his brother Bobby was the attorney general of the United States.

During a televised debate, McCormack attacked Kennedy by saying the Senate seat should be filled on merit, not on inheritance, that if his opponent's name were Edward Moore instead of Edward Moore Kennedy no one would pay any attention to him. Luckily, however, voters seemed to feel that all of McCormack's nasty campaign comments were out of line, and in September of that year, Teddy defeated McCormack by a two-to-one margin.

In the November special election, Teddy defeated the Republican candidate, George Cabot Lodge II, who was from another powerful Massachusetts political family, with fifty-three percent of the vote.

On November 7, 1962, Teddy was sworn in to the Senate. It was a proud moment for him—and for his family. The boy that no one expected much from was now a United States Senator.

Still, Teddy couldn't escape being compared to his brothers. He lacked Jack's sophistication, some said, while others said there was none of Bobby's intense drive in him. He forged ahead, working as hard as he could, avoiding publicity and focusing on committee work and local Massachusetts issues. He was also deferential toward the older Senators from the South who seemed to run everything. The one adjective that most people used to describe Teddy during this time was "affable."

Everything changed on November 22, 1963. An aide rushed up to him on the floor of the Senate to tell him that Jack had been shot during a motorcade in Dallas, Texas. Teddy left the Senate floor immediately to find Bobby, who soon afterward informed him that Jack was dead.

Within minutes, Teddy managed to pull himself together, so he could fly up to Hyannis Port to tell his father, now suffering from a stroke, that his second son, the President of the United States, was dead.

The Senate and the Death of a Third Brother

Less than a year later, on June 19, 1964, Teddy was a passenger in a private plane flying from Washington, DC, to western Massachusetts, when the pilot encountered severe weather as it neared the Barnes Airport. The plane crashed into an apple orchard, killing the pilot and Edward Moss, who was one of Teddy's

Senate aides. Teddy himself was pulled unconscious from the wreckage by Birch Bayh II, a fellow Senator.

Emergency vehicles were on the scene almost immediately, and Teddy was transported to a nearby hospital. Doctors discovered a punctured lung, broken ribs, and internal bleeding. His back was also severely injured, and he would have chronic back pain for the rest of his life.

After Teddy was released from the hospital, he was ordered by his family physician to remain at home to convalesce from his injuries. During this time, Teddy was able to meet with various authorities on a variety of issues he was interested in so he could study them more closely. The hospital experiences he had during this time also contributed greatly to a lifelong interest in making sure all Americans received the medical treatment they needed and, Teddy believed, deserved.

Since Teddy was not physically able to

campaign for the regular 1964 Senate election to retain his seat representing Massachusetts, Joan campaigned for him and surprised everyone with her political skills. That November, Teddy defeated his opponent by a three-to-one margin.

In January 1965, Teddy returned to the Senate, but now he was using a cane to help him walk. The men and women who had come to his home while he was convalescing had told him that he needed to have a stronger and more proactive staff around him, so he took their advice and hired some of the best minds he could find.

That year, he almost single-handedly succeeded in amending the Voting Rights Bill to ban the poll tax, which was used mostly in Southern States to keep African-Americans from voting. In doing so, Teddy gained a reputation for legislative skills that would only grow stronger in the coming years. He also showed by his actions that he wasn't afraid to oppose President Lyndon B. Johnson.

That year, too, along with other senators, Teddy fought to push through the Immigration and Nationality Act of 1965, the purpose of which was to get rid of a quota system that was based on a person's country of origin.

During this time, Teddy, following Jack's line of thinking, showed no inclination against expanding the role of the United States in the war raging in Vietnam. To him, just as it had been with Jack, the war was a struggle to contain Communism and, as such, it might last for many years.

Teddy was bothered by the plight of Vietnamese refugees, though, and in the Senate, when he held hearings about their plight, he discovered that the government had absolutely no policy at all for dealing with them. Teddy also thought the draft was unfair because it allowed for wealthy and well connected young men, mostly white, to get deferments, especially to stay in college, while those who were poor or belonged to minorities had no such options.

Teddy and Joan's third child, their second son, Patrick Joseph Kennedy, was born on July 14, 1967.

In January 1968, Teddy toured Vietnam to see for himself what was happening there. He came back totally disillusioned by the United States military's lack of progress in the war and by the all-pervasive corruption of the government of South Vietnam. He stated publically that South Vietnam should be told either to put their house in order or the United States would leave them to fend for themselves against the North Vietnamese forces.

Teddy knew that Bobby, now a Senator representing New York, wanted to challenge Lyndon Johnson for the 1968 Democratic Party nomination, but he advised his brother against doing such a thing. It was certainly no secret that the Kennedy family thought

Johnson was a crude, deceitful, and ruthless man, and that they resented the fact that he had fallen into the presidency because of the death of their beloved Jack.

Still, Teddy believed he had learned enough about how politics really worked to know that a challenge by Bobby of a sitting president of the same political party could seriously backfire and damage the political aspirations of them both.

But when Senator Eugene McCarthy from Minnesota had a very strong showing in the New Hampshire Democratic primary, running on an anti–Vietnam War platform, President Lyndon Johnson was so despondent he announced that he would not seek another term. Now, the race to become the Democratic candidate was wide open, so in March of that year Bobby began his own campaign for the presidency.

Once again, Teddy flew around the Western states, as he had done for Jack, this time recruiting delegates to support Bobby's presidential aspirations.

On June 4, Teddy was in San Francisco when Bobby won a crucial victory in the California primary. It was a joyous occasion, and Teddy told several of the campaign staffers with him that he had no doubt now, even though Bobby was still significantly behind one of the other Democratic Party primary candidates, Hubert Humphrey, also from Minnesota, that his brother would be the second Kennedy man in the White House.

Just after midnight on June 5, though, after a jubilant celebration of the California win, Bobby was shot by a twenty-four-year-old Palestinian immigrant named Sirhan Sirhan.

Teddy was devastated, because among all of his brothers and sisters, he was closest to Bobby. People who saw Teddy at the hospital standing by Bobby in his last hours told their family and friends that they had never before seen more grief in one person's face than they saw on Teddy's face that night.

Bobby's body lay in state at St. Patrick's Cathedral in New York City for two days until the funeral mass was held on June 8. Teddy delivered the eulogy. Bobby was buried in Arlington National Cemetery near Jack's grave.

The Democratic National Convention was held that August in Chicago. It was chaotic for many reasons. Antiwar protesters confronted the Chicago police daily. Television viewers more often saw pitched battles and arrests outside the convention hall than they did the political events taking place inside. But even those events were more contentious than usual. Richard J. Daley, the powerful mayor of Chicago and a force in the Democratic Party, feared that Hubert Humphrey was too weak to unite the party, so he tried to convince Teddy that he should make himself available for a draft nomination from the floor. Daley made sure that

"Draft Ted" movements sprang up among delegates all over the convention hall.

Teddy wanted no part of this movement, though, and he resented what Daley was trying to pull. He knew he was not ready to become the leader of the most powerful nation on earth, and he was sure that for all of the delegates present he was merely a stand-in for both Jack and Bobby. Teddy turned down every attempt to place his name before the convention as a candidate. He even declined to be nominated for the vice presidential spot on the ticket. Bobby's disappointed delegates had to settle for Senator George McGovern to be their voice in the convention.

Now that Teddy was the only brother alive, he was not only the father to his three children, but he became the surrogate father for Jack's two children, Caroline and John Jr., and to Bobby's eleven children: Kathleen, Joseph, Robert Jr., David, Mary Courtney, Michael, Mary Kerry, Christopher, Matthew, Douglas, and Rory.

After Richard Nixon was elected president in November, it was widely assumed by everyone that Teddy would be the Democratic Party's candidate for the 1972 presidential election.

In January 1969, Teddy became Senate majority whip, the youngest person ever to attain that position, after he defeated Senator Russell Long by a 31–26 vote. The whip ensures control of the formal decision-making process.

On the surface, things seemed to be going very well for Teddy, and, incredibly, the son whom no one in the family initially expected anything great from, could possibly become the next president of the United States. But doubts that he would be able to succeed in such a powerful position continually plagued Teddy.

On November 18, 1969, Teddy's father, Joseph Patrick Kennedy Sr., died at the age of eighty-one.

In 1970, Teddy won reelection to another Senate term. Although he received sixty-two percent of the vote against Republican candidate Josiah Spaulding, it was about a half million fewer votes than he had received in the 1964 election.

By January 1971, Teddy had lost some of his support in the Senate and was defeated by Senator Robert Byrd of West Virginia, 31–24, for the position of Senate majority whip.

Later, Teddy would tell Byrd that it was a blessing in disguise, because it allowed him to focus on where he was strongest, working on current issues and serving on committees. Along with Senator Jacob Javits of New York, Teddy played a very important role in the passage of the National Cancer Act that year.

In October of that year, Teddy made his first speech about the violence in Northern Ireland, telling everyone that Ulster, the British name for the area, was becoming Britain's Vietnam, and he demanded the removal of all British troops and the reunification of the two Irelands. He ended the speech by saying that all of the Protestants in Ulster should find a way to return to Britain.

The British government was furious. Although Teddy retracted the part of his speech about Ulster's Protestants, he formed a strong relationship with John Hume, the founder of the Irish Social Democratic and Labour Party.

Teddy also began to give anti–Vietnam War speeches anywhere he had the chance. He especially opposed Nixon's policy called "Vietnamization," which he believed would lead to an even longer and more violent war.

In December of that year, Teddy attacked the Nixon administration again, this time for its support of West Pakistan's (now simply known as Pakistan) army in the brutal repression of the people of East Pakistan, the Bengali area, separated from the West Pakistan by India. West Pakistan's actions precipitated a war of independence and in 1971 East Pakistan became the independent country of Bangladesh. In February 1972,

Teddy flew to the country to deliver a speech at Dhaka University, the site of a killing rampage a year earlier.

Although Teddy had declared that he would not be a candidate in the 1972 United States presidential election, national polls were telling the party faithful that if Teddy tried, the nomination was his. Ever aware of who he was, Teddy gave some serious thought to running, but in the end he decided that not only did he need more experience, he also wanted to make sure his children and the children of his two brothers were taken care of.

At the Democratic Party National Convention that year, as George McGovern was inching closer and closer to the magic number for nomination, anti-McGovern forces once again tried to get Teddy to let them put his name in nomination from the floor. And once again, Teddy declined. Teddy also turned down McGovern's attempt to recruit him as his running mate. Instead, Teddy's brother-in-law,

Sargent Shriver, Eunice's husband, accepted the vice presidential nomination.

That next year, 1973, Teddy and Joan's son Edward Jr. had part of his right leg amputated because of cancer, and afterward underwent a difficult two-year rehabilitation treatment. Half a year later, Edward Jr.'s return to the ski slopes on his artificial leg brought national attention to how successful the amputation and rehabilitation treatment had been.

Around the same time, Teddy and Joan's other son, Patrick, was suffering from severe asthma attacks. The continued stress of Teddy's political career, with all of its ups and downs, and the health problems of their two sons, finally had its affect on Joan. Several times, she checked herself into hospitals to be treated for emotional strain.

During this time, Teddy resurrected his efforts for national health insurance. Although he supported the single-payer option that organized labor wanted, Teddy also negotiated with the Nixon White House on what it wanted, a type of employer-based, HMO (Health Maintenance Options) solution. The two sides could never reach a compromise, though, and Teddy eventually gave up trying, although he admitted later that that was a mistake.

On June 17, 1972, five men connected to President Richard Nixon's presidential campaign broke into Democratic National Committee headquarters at the Watergate complex on the banks of the Potomac River in Washington, DC. Investigations by the Senate Watergate Committee, the House Judiciary Committee, and the national and international news media eventually led to Nixon's resignation on August 9, 1974. Nixon's vice president, Gerald Ford, assumed the presidency. He would later issue a full pardon for the former president.

In the wake of the Watergate scandal,

Teddy became a major force behind the passage of the Federal Election Campaign Act Amendments of 1974, which would establish public financing for presidential elections and limit how much money individuals could contribute.

In April of the next year, Teddy traveled to the Soviet Union for talks with the country's leader, Leonid Brezhnev, where he advocated a full nuclear test ban as well as lifting emigration restrictions for Soviet citizens.

At the end of that month, Saigon, the capital of South Vietnam, fell to the North Vietnamese army, but Teddy, through his Subcommittee on Refugees and Escapees, continued to focus on the problems he knew the war, although over for all intents and purposes, was still creating.

Once again, with the 1976 presidential elections looming, Teddy's name was talked about, but articles in several major newspapers and magazines raised doubts.

In September 1974, Teddy announced again that he would not be a presidential candidate and that his decision was final. The eventual Democratic candidate, a relatively unknown politician from Georgia, Jimmy Carter, did nothing to build a relationship with Teddy and the Kennedy family. In fact, he seemed to go out of his way to make sure there was no connection whatsoever.

Teddy was also up for reelection that year for his Senate seat, and he had a challenger in the Democratic primary, a man who was angry at Teddy for supporting bussing in Boston to integrate the school system. Again, he easily defeated his opponent and then won the November general election for the seat with seventy-four percent of the vote.

The Carter years in the White House were some of Teddy's least successful years as a politician. Where once he had been one of the most powerful politicians in Washington, Teddy now seemed almost at a loss at what he should do. Although he and Carter shared similar ideologies, they had different priorities, and Carter didn't seem interested in pushing the idea of a national health insurance.

Teddy and Joan separated in 1978, although they would often join each other at various public events, where it seemed proper for Teddy to have her by his side.

In 1979, Teddy did become chair of the Senate Judiciary Committee, but that year, he also had another falling out with Carter on the issue of a national health insurance.

A poll taken in the middle of the summer of 1979 showed that Democrats preferred Teddy to Carter by a three-to-one margin. Carter announced that he wasn't intimidated by his twenty-eight percent approval rating and that if Teddy decided to run against him for the Democratic Party nomination he'd easily beat him.

The Lion of the Senate

In August 1979 Carter's approval rating had plummeted to twenty-eight percent. When national polls showed that Teddy could beat Carter in a presidential race by a two-to-one margin, Teddy decided he was ready to take on the challenge. On November 7, he formally announced his campaign at Boston's Faneuil Hall. Shortly after that, though, in a television interview with CBS News's Roger

Mudd, Teddy's rambling and at times almost incoherent response to the question, "Why do you want to be President?" brought about a lot of negative reviews.

Some news outlets even brought up personal and public scandal, but this time Teddy wouldn't be discouraged. He truly believed that Carter's difficult first term in office and his extremely low approval rating could easily give control of the government to the Republican Party again.

Teddy made no secret of the fact that he planned to criticize, often and publicly, what he saw as a total failure of the Carter administration. He had never forgiven Carter for his calculated detachment from "the Washington crowd" and for refusing to "play the political game." One thing Teddy did promise, though, was that if Carter eventually became the Democratic Party's candidate, he would support him.

As it turned out, Teddy only won ten of

the nation's primaries. Still, Teddy carried his campaign to the 1980 Democratic National Convention in New York that August. It was his hope that he could get a rule passed that would free delegates from their being bound by the results of their state primaries, and thereby open up the convention.

When this move failed on the first night, Teddy withdrew his nomination, but on the second night, August 12, he gave the most important speech of his life. He quoted Martin Luther King Jr., Franklin Delano Roosevelt, and Alfred Lord Tennyson that American liberalism was not a thing of the past, that the hope for a truly united and integrated America would never die.

That November, the Republican candidate, Ronald Reagan, was elected the fortieth president of the United States. As the 1980s transpired, the sweeping changes in government that Reagan campaigned for began to be implemented, and Teddy's brand of liberalism soon began to lose favor, even with mainstream Democrats.

Those years were extremely difficult for Teddy. It was hard for him to comprehend that he was a member of the minority party. He couldn't understand how the people of any nation, let alone the United States, could swing so violently back and forth ideologically. Teddy had always believed what he still believed. How could Reagan's view of how the world should be suddenly appeal to so many people?

Feeling almost useless in the Senate, Teddy also began to face more serious problems in his personal life. Although they had been officially separated for several years, in 1982, after twenty-four years of marriage, Teddy and Joan finally divorced.

For the next decade, Teddy seemed to wander through life without a compass. There were more and more stories of struggles in his private life. In spite of these, though, he won reelection to the Senate in 1982 and again in 1988. Still, after eight years of Ronald Reagan, another Republican, George Herbert Walker Bush, was elected the forty-first president in 1988 and served from 1989 until 1993.

Finally, in 1992, Teddy married Victoria Reggie, whose family had been friends with the Kennedy family for years. On many occasions, Teddy told friends and family that he credited his full recovery to his relationship with Victoria.

When Bill Clinton returned the Democrats to the White House in 1992, the Republicans had owned the White House for twelve years. Clinton made no secret of his admiration for the Kennedy family. In fact, a photograph of him shaking hands with President John F. Kennedy was one of his most cherished possessions. Now, Teddy once again became an influential legislator and could restart his push for health-care reform.

On January 22, 1995, Rose Fitzgerald

Kennedy, Teddy's mother, died at the age of 104.

In 1996, Teddy authored the Health Insurance Portability and Accountability Act. This allowed people who change or lose their jobs to maintain health insurance. The act also protected the privacy of a patient's medical information. In 1997, Teddy helped create the State Children's Health Insurance Program, now called CHIP. This increased health care coverage of children eighteen years old and under.

Teddy had once again become one of the Senate's most prominent members. He was able to pass a record number of legislative bills that changed the lives of Americans of all socioeconomic levels. Teddy sponsored legislation in criminal code reform, public education, immigration reform, fair housing, health care, and AIDS research.

Wanting to be true to his liberal principals, but knowing that it would take a supreme effort to convince some of his more conservative colleagues to join him, Teddy, through political skill and bipartisan friendships, was able to get a consensus among all of the members of the Senate Judiciary Committee to uphold liberal positions on various issues. He even teamed up with such conservative Senators as Nancy Kassebaum, John McCain, and Orrin Hatch to cosponsor legislation on immigration, funding for traumatic brain injuries, and healthcare benefits for all workers.

George W. Bush, the son of George H.W. Bush, became the forty-third president after winning a contested election in 2000.

As America came into the new millennium, with the Democrats now out of power again, Teddy continued to work with both Democrats and Republican to pass the No Child Left Behind Act, an attempt to close the achievement gap in the nation's public schools.

After the attacks of September 11, 2001, Teddy oversaw the coordination effort to make sure that all government agencies charged with helping people in catastrophic emergencies could also respond to the mental health needs of the victims' families. In addition, he helped sponsor the Bioterrorism Preparedness and Response Act, the aim of which was to prevent, prepare for, and respond to bioterrorism emergencies.

As a nonsupporter of the war in Iraq, Teddy sponsored legislation meant to send more armored Humvees to the battle zone to help protect troops against roadside bombs.

On January 7, 2005, Teddy's sister Rosemary died in a residential-care facility in Wisconsin, where she had been for sixty-four years.

On September 17, 2006, Teddy's sister Patricia died in Manhattan.

In the years that followed, Teddy either sponsored or cosponsored legislation that would help law enforcement agencies to rescue and then protect abducted children, would reauthorize the Individuals with Disabilities Education Act, and would expand Medicaid coverage.

On May 17, 2008, Teddy suffered a seizure and was taken to Cape Cod Hospital in Hyannis. Doctors discovered that he had a growth in his brain, a malignant glioma, an especially lethal type of cancer. Right before Teddy underwent surgery on June 2, he made a statement to the press that he was deeply grateful, humbled, and strengthened by the letters of support and well wishes he had received from the people of Massachusetts, from his friends and his colleagues, and from people all around the world.

When the surgery was over, the doctors pronounced it a success and said that in their collective opinions Teddy would have no permanent neurological effects from the removal of the cancerous tissue.

Initially, there didn't seem to be, and during the 2008 presidential primaries, Teddy endorsed Senator Barack Obama's candidacy, much to the chagrin of the Clintons, who had been counting on Teddy's endorsement of Hillary's candidacy.

When the Democratic primaries were over, Barack Obama had the requisite number of votes to make him the party's candidate for the 2008 presidential election. At the Democratic Party Convention in Denver, Teddy made an emotional appearance. He looked physically weak, but his eyes shone with excitement at the nomination of the nation's first black candidate, and he delivered a short but rousing speech to the delegates on the floor.

On September 26, Teddy suffered a mild seizure while he was at his home in Hyannis Port. He was examined by his doctors and released from the hospital the same day. They felt that a change in Teddy's medicine was what had triggered the seizure.

That November, Barack Obama easily

defeated Senator John McCain, the Republican candidate, to return the Democratic Party to power after eight years of Republican Party rule under George W. Bush.

During Barack Obama's post-inauguration luncheon at the United States Capitol on January 20, 2009, Teddy suffered another seizure and was quickly rushed to a hospital by paramedics. This time Teddy was accompanied by Senators John Kerry, Chris Dodd, and Orrin Hatch. Later in the day, Teddy's doctor released a statement saying he believed that what had happened to Teddy was simply a matter of fatigue brought on by all of the events surrounding the inauguration.

After resting in Florida for a few weeks, Teddy returned to the Senate to vote for its version of the economic stimulus package, telling his colleagues that he had come to the Senate that day to do all he could to support President Obama and his plan to get the country back on track by acting quickly and boldly, and yet responsibly, to stimulate the economy.

By June, though, Teddy hadn't cast a Senate vote in over four months. His health had forced him to stay in Massachusetts, where he was undergoing rounds of chemotherapy. In his absence, the health care reform that the Democrats in both the House and the Senate wanted to pass seemed to be getting nowhere without Teddy's ability to achieve bipartisan support on such bills.

In July, a health care reform bill which Teddy favored was approved by a Senate committee, but all his old friends told him that it faced a long, difficult road ahead before it would ever become law.

When Teddy's sister Eunice died on August 11, he attended a private service, but he was too ill to attend the public service.

On August 20, Teddy made a sudden request of the governor of Massachusetts to change a state law to allow the governor to appoint a successor to his Senate seat immediately upon his death, instead of having to hold a special election that could take several months. Teddy wanted to make sure there were enough votes in the Senate to pass health reform legislation.

Teddy died of brain cancer on Tuesday, August 25, 2009, at his home in Hyannis Port. People lined the streets of the town, the roads leading to Boston, and the streets of Boston itself to see the hearse carrying their beloved Senator.

Teddy's funeral mass was watched by millions of people around the world. In a letter revealed after his death, Teddy had asked Pope Benedict XVI to pray for him. It is easy to believe that he was remembering how, as a boy of seven in 1939, he had received his first communion from Pope Pius XII.

As a child, Teddy was, at best, an afterthought, and in the beginning no one expected anything of him. Yet at the end, although he would never had uttered such words, he had achieved more than his other brothers combined.

As of August 25, 2009, the Lion of the United States Senate would roar no more.